THE PERFECT NANNY

AN ADDICTIVE AND GRIPPING PSYCHOLOGICAL THRILLER

AARON QUINN

Published by aaronquinnbooks.com

Copyright @ Aaron Quinn 2024

All rights reserved.

Aaron Quinn has asserted his right to be identified as the author of this work.

No part of this book may be reproduced, stored in any retrieval system, or transmitted in any form or by any means, electronic, mechanical, photocopying, recording or otherwise, without the prior written permission of the author.

This book is a work of fiction, names, characters, businesses, organisations, places and events other than those clearly in the public domain, are either the product of the author's imagination or used fictitiously. Any resemblance to actual persons, living or dead, events or locales is entirely coincidental.

I knew something wasn't right the moment she walked through the door, but I couldn't have imagined how far she was willing to go.

1

LUCY

The laughter of my children, Sarah and Matthew, echoes off the walls as they chase each other round the house, their footsteps thundering like a stampede of wild elephants. Toys scatter across the floor in their wake, remnants of a day filled with carefree play.

"Kids, be careful," I call out, wiping down the kitchen counter with a damp cloth. Chaos seems to follow them wherever they go. My eyes drift to the family pictures that hang from the walls, capturing moments of happiness—beach holidays, picnics in the park, birthdays celebrated with friends. "Sarah, Matthew, slow down will you before you break something." My voice rises with concern. Because of their endless energy, they've left a trail of mess in the kitchen that I'm trying to tidy up.

"Sorry, Mum," they chime in unison, giggling as they skid to a halt outside the doorway. With their flushed faces and eyes sparkling with mischief, it's impossible not to smile back at them.

"Right, you two." I shake my head in mock exasperation. "Try to not wreck the house, okay? Or you'll be in bed before you know it."

"Promise," they reply before racing off again, their laughter filling the air. Matthew is nine, confident and protective of his five-year-old little sister, who's a princess in the making. He takes Sarah by the hand, his pace so fast that she has a hard time keeping up as her little pencil-like legs scurry along.

As I finish clearing the last of the debris from the kitchen, I think about how lucky I am to have such happy kids. And yet, sometimes I feel trapped, confined within these walls with my mundane daily routine. I miss the thrill of my career, and the satisfaction that comes from making decisions that impact more than just our little family. I long for the excitement, the sense of purpose that once filled my days.

The sound of the front door opening interrupts my thoughts, followed by a familiar voice calling out, "Hello. Where are my children? Has the green bogey monster eaten them up?"

"Daddy!" The children's screams cut through my reverie, and I lean against the kitchen counter, watching as they race to greet their dad. I should be happy, but again I'm filled with an unexpected sadness that washes over me. Greg's homecoming should fill me with pleasure and ease, yet here I stand, drowned in a sea of melancholy, as the laughter of my children echoes like a reminder of the life I've paused.

"Hey, there you are." Greg scoops them up into his strong arms and spins them round. I smile at the sight. As their laughter dies down, Greg looks over at me, brow furrowed in concern. "You okay, Luce?" he asks, setting the kids down.

The Perfect Nanny 3

"Fine," I force a smile. "Just thinking, I guess."

"Ah." His expression shifts to one of understanding mixed with mild annoyance. He sighs and tuts, rubbing the back of his neck. "Every week, it's the same conversation. What more do you expect me to say?"

I chew my lip as I search for the right words. "I miss my old job sometimes, you know? The excitement, the challenge. I feel like I've lost a part of myself since becoming a full-time mum. Every time you walk through that door I'm reminded of the freedom you enjoy. Think about it... You go out most days. You wine and dine clients in Cambridge till the early hours of the morning. You get away to the gym three days a week and you hang back to have a coffee and catch-up with Dave, Alex, and Nasheed. What do I do? Stare at these walls is what I do. I also cook, clean, and iron. I hardly go out *anywhere* and the most challenging thing I face each week is wondering what to put on our weekly Tesco's shopping list. Whoopie me."

Greg sighs, running a hand through his hair. "Lucy, we've talked about this so many times. I think you're doing an amazing job taking care of our kids, and I don't want to see you give that up. And besides, I make enough money to cover both of our salaries many times over and my business is growing year-on-year."

I know all of that. And everything Greg has mentioned is true, but money isn't the problem. Greg's approaching thirty-five in a few months and owns an advertising design agency—which comes with long hours and high-profile clients, but it affords us a very good lifestyle with two cars, all-inclusive holidays, and the opportunity to buy anything for the house without worrying about how we'll pay it off.

"Christ, Greg, I'm not saying I want to abandon them,

and it's not about the money either," I protest, my voice rising in frustration. "But why can't I have both? My old career back and a family?"

"Because it's not what's best for our children." He crosses his arms over his chest. Ready to dig in. Ready to discount my needs in favour of his own. "They need stability, someone who's always there for them. And if you go back to work, that won't be possible."

Since the first time Greg and I spoke about having a family of our own, he made his thoughts about bringing up the kids clear, and he was quite vocal about it. Having a nanny was a legacy in his family. Greg had one and his dad did, too. So, it was something very natural for them to consider. Secretly, I hoped Greg would go off the idea of me being home full-time like his mum and grandma when he saw how much I was earning as a senior buyer for a clothing retailer in London. But as the years passed, he stayed as resolute about his feelings about me staying at home.

"Maybe we could hire help," I suggest. "A nanny or childminder to ease the burden."

"I'm not keen on that idea." My husband's face hardens.

"Then what do you expect me to do?" I demand.

"Lucy—," he begins, but I cut him off.

"Never mind," I say. "We clearly have differing opinions."

"Fine," Greg replies, his jaw clenched.

"Hey, guys." He turns to the kids who are still lurking in the hallway, his voice warm as he ruffles their hair. "How was your day?"

"Happy!" exclaims Sarah, her eyes sparkling. "We made a fort with the cushions."

The Perfect Nanny

"Did you? I hope you left enough room for me?" Greg laughs, hoisting Matthew onto his shoulders.

"Please, Greg," I implore, desperation making my words tremble. "I can't do this on my own. I need my old life back. I spoke this morning to Lynne Mitchell, my old Buying Director. It was a catch up of sorts."

Greg pulls a tight smile. "Oh, right. How's everything in the business?"

My heart flutters in my chest. I've thought about the conversation all day, and now's a good a time as any to sound Greg out. "It's good. Very good. Lynne mentioned that their current buyer for outwear is leaving on maternity leave and she wondered if I'd like a temporary contract to cover."

Greg folds his arms and studies me in silence.

I continue to fill the void before he can say anything. "Lynne said I have a better relationship with our Far East suppliers than anyone else in the business, so the transition to pick up with my old contacts would be easy."

"Luce…"

I hold my hand up to stop him. "Let me finish. Lynne said I can work from home a few days a week. So having a nanny part-time would mean I could still be available for the kids even if the nanny is here. This trial is a win-win for me, us, and Lynne. She said if it gets too much for me then she'd find a replacement and employ me as a remote consultant." There, I've said it now. My mouth is parched, my hands are sweaty, and my chest feels tight. "Please Greg…"

He studies me, his expression softening slightly. "Alright," he relents, the word heavy with resignation. "We'll look into hiring childcare help."

"Really?" My face lights up, relief flooding through me like a tidal wave. "That would make such a difference."

"Let's hope we find someone we can trust," he mutters, unenthusiastic about the idea.

"Of course." I step away and reach for the fridge door to pull out a bottle of white wine before filling a glass for Greg as he only drinks white, and I grab a red from the larder for me as it's my favourite. I hand him his glass. "We'll find the perfect candidate."

As we sit down in the lounge, Greg leans back in his chair. "You know, Lucy," he begins, clearly not sold on the idea yet, "there are pros and cons to having a nanny versus you staying at home with the kids."

"Like what?" A sinking feeling hits the bottom of my stomach, and the thought that Greg's going to go back on his word.

"Well," he starts, his brow furrowing, "a nanny could give you the freedom to pursue your career again, but it also means trusting our children's safety and well-being to someone else. What if something goes wrong?"

"I understand." My fingers knot together in my lap. "But we'll interview and check all references. Besides," I pause, taking a deep breath, "we're not the first parents to hire help, are we? Surely there are good nannies out there? And your family has done it in the past."

"True," he concedes, "but don't forget about the costs. A qualified nanny won't come cheap. And then there's the emotional aspect." He hesitates, searching for the right words. "The kids might feel abandoned or get attached to the nanny instead of us." Greg's eyes locked on mine, as if trying to gauge my resolve. "Alright. We'll try it. But," he raises a finger, "if anything feels off or if the kids seem unhappy, we have to sit down and consider other options."

"Deal," I agree, relief washing over me. The clink of our glasses echo. Greg's hazel eyes twinkle with amusement as we share stories of our past lives—a time before dirty nappies and sleepless nights.

"Remember that holiday in Spain, when we got lost on the way to the restaurant?" The memory coaxes a grin. Then I roll my eyes and stare at the ceiling as he recalls the night we stumbled upon a tiny bar and ended up dancing with local folk who wouldn't let us sneak off until we'd fully embarrassed ourselves. I lean back in my chair, my laughter mingling with his. Finally, the tension that has been suffocating our relationship seems to have lessened. "Those were the days. I miss them sometimes," I sigh, sipping from my glass, savouring the sharpness as the liquid strokes my tongue.

"Me too." He reaches across to squeeze my hand. "But we've got something even better now." Our children giggle at their favourite movie as Greg gestures toward them. "And we'll make it work, somehow."

"Time for bed, you two. You've got school tomorrow," I call out, standing up.

"Aw, Mum. Ten more minutes, please?" Sarah whines, her blue eyes pleading with me.

"Please, Mum?" Matthew chimes in, his brown curls bouncing as he nods. "We promise we'll go straight to bed after that."

"Alright." I relent. "Ten more minutes. But not a second longer, understood?"

"Thank you, Mummy," they say together, their faces lighting up with delight.

A knock at the door startles me from the moment. Beth, our neighbour, her wavy red hair framing her concerned blue eyes, stands on our doorstep. "Hey, Lucy. I'm not disturbing you, am I? I wanted to drop off cupcakes I baked for the kids. How are you doing?"

"Thanks, Beth." I force a smile, accept the warm box

filled with sweet delights and usher my friend into the kitchen. "I'm alright. We've been discussing my going back to work and hiring a nanny for the kids."

"Really?" Her eyebrows shoot up in surprise. "That's quite a change, Lucy. If you need anything, I'd be happy to help. Might be a good laugh."

"Thank you." Relief washes over me. Beth is good at brainstorming, far better at it than me. She's a forty something divorcee and a freelance social media marketing consultant. A snazzy title for someone who works from home in her PJs helping clients to boost their social media presence with innovative strategies. It amazes me how her mind works. I hate social media and stick to posting usual stuff like days out with the family, eating out, and family get togethers. "That would mean a lot." As we chat, I get Beth up to speed with my plans to go back to work and what we've decided about hiring a part-time nanny. Greg emerges from the shadows, his stern features betraying his reluctance.

"I have a little work to finish and then I'm getting an early night." He glances at me before heading to the study. "I trust you, Luce. I know you'll be able to figure out a good approach for vetting the candidates. Can you come up with some cracking questions?"

His words stun me a bit, along with his ability to compartmentalise and delegate family matters to me. Instead of letting it get to me, I focus on Beth's offer of help. She's always been there for us, even when Greg wants to be a dictator instead of a partner. We've been friends and neighbours for a few years now and get on so well. Beth's a brilliant listener and for her sins, my sounding board. She hates conflict like me and wants to get along with everyone. But she's a lot like me and gets emotional when stressed.

The Perfect Nanny

A hush falls over the room as Beth and I settle down at the kitchen table, its surface cluttered with papers and the remnants of our dinner. The scent of red wine lingers in the air, mingling with the fading aroma of roast chicken. My heart races, a mixture of anxiety and excitement building within me. This is it, the beginning of my journey back to the career I've missed for so long.

"Alright." Beth's voice is soft but steady. "Let's start with the job ad."

I agree, picking up a pen and tapping it against my chin, my mind racing with thoughts. What are the qualities I want in a nanny? Someone kind, patient, experienced… someone who will care about my children as much as I do. Someone who will treat them like their own. "Must have," I scribble, "at least five years' experience, excellent references, and a passion for child development."

"Good," Beth eyes scan the words, "and add something about being able to handle emergencies and having a flexible schedule?"

"Right. Good shout," I add the extra stuff, "anything else we should include?"

"Let's not forget," she raises an eyebrow playfully, "they'll need to tolerate Greg's stubbornness and not be too attractive or they might take their nannying duties a touch too far if he's round."

We share a laugh. "Okay," I take a deep breath, "on to interview questions." Together we jot down a ton of questions, weeding out the irrelevant ones after a break and a copious top-up of red wine. As the hours wear on, exhaustion creeps in, tugging at our eyelids and dulling our thoughts. "Alright," I finally say, my voice thick with fatigue and slurred from the wine as we gather up my notes. "I think we've got everything covered." I hug Beth at the front door. "Catch up tomorrow."

As I climb the stairs to bed, my head spins with the weight of decisions that lie ahead. And as I lay down beside Greg, his steady breathing a comfort in the darkness, I wonder—will this choice bring us closer together or tear us apart? Only time will tell.

2

LUCY

Three days have passed since I drew up the shortlist for our new nanny. With the help of the agency, we shortlisted a bunch of potential applicants. Greg and I blitzed through them over short fifteen-minute Zoom calls to get a feel for them. Not only was it insightful but saved us a ton of time seeing them face-to-face and putting the kids through a merry-go-round of informal introductions. We were left with three potentials to meet in person before making our final decision.

Determined to make a good impression on the candidates, I tidy the house and clear away my children's toys. I don't think my hoover has ever seen so much action, and the can of Mr Sheen is nearly empty as I race round dusting all the surfaces. With each passing minute, I can feel the stress mounting as a tight ball of anxiety grips my stomach. The lounge looks like a storm swept through it, but I wipe the fine sheen of sweat from my brow and push on. I want the whole house to look perfect, clean, and stylish.

"Right, this goes there, and that should be... over here," I mutter, organising the toys into neat piles.

"Lucy, deep breaths." Greg's voice snaps me from my thoughts. He stands in the doorway, watching me with a wince etched on his face. "Remember, we're doing the interviews together."

"Yes, I know, Greg. But you know me, I want everything to be perfect." I force a smile. But inside, the doubt gnaws at me. What if none of them are right? What if they don't like us, or worse, the kids don't like them? If my sole chance to reclaim my career and carve out something special for myself slipped away, it would leave me utterly shattered.

"Kids," Greg calls out. Sarah and Matthew appear, their faces showing a mixture of curiosity and apprehension. Greg crouches down to their level. "I need you both to be on your best behaviour today, alright? We're going to meet a few potential nannies, and we want them to see how lovely you two can be."

"Okay, Daddy." Sarah nods. Matthew echoes her response, though I can tell he's less than thrilled about the prospect of a stranger in our home.

Greg looks up at me and I give him a grateful look. He offers a reassuring smile in return.

Having finished the dusting, I fluff pillows and rearrange the coffee table. "Alright," I tell myself, taking a deep breath as I take one last look round my lounge, which has never looked this clean and tidy. "We're ready."

The doorbell rings not long after, and I feel my heartbeat quicken.

"First one's here." Greg walks towards the front door. I stand up straight, smoothing my outfit before following him.

After my husband opens the door, I regard the woman

standing there. The first candidate has a warm smile and kind eyes. "Hello, I'm Jane." She holds out a hand as she introduces herself.

Greg invites her inside and we take our places in the lounge. As she speaks with us, I note her experience. Jane came across strong on Zoom and with an interesting CV was very vocal in the video call, but as she sits in front of us, I spot her clench and unclench her right hand. Nerves possibly? I try to ignore it, but I can't stop my eyes from wandering down to her hand. The more she does it, the more annoying it is to the point that I want to march over to her seat and sit on her hand. And then it hits me. The smell. Slight at first but becomes stronger over the next minute or so. I look across at Greg, and I can tell he's noticed it too as he smiles awkwardly. She's bloody farted... and on my sofa too. The hand clenching! She was trying to hold it in. Jesus!

"Thank you for coming, Jane," I tell her as we wrap up the interview quickly without appearing rude. "We'll be in touch."

"Looking forward to it," she replies as he jumps up with another smile before leaving, clutching her coat in one hand, and her handbag and file in the other. She can't get out of the door quick enough.

I look at Greg after he closes the door and we both burst out in laughter. "I feel sick." I pull a face of disgust.

"Not as sick as her guts. At least she didn't follow through."

I groan and gag at Greg's comment as I rush to the kitchen to get some air freshener spray.

After a while, the second candidate arrives. Karen appears promising on paper, but something about her demeanour puts me on edge. I'm not sure what it is. Call it a sixth sense or women's intuition, but I don't warm to her.

She says all the right things, looks the part, and does a grand job of engaging with us... perhaps a bit too much, and laughs at things with such a shrill that it would wake the dead at a mortuary.

The interview soon takes a turn for the worse when she throws a grenade of a question.

"Discipline and punishment are essential for a child's development so they know right from wrong. Being firm is essential to enforce boundaries. As parents, how do you deal with disobedience and what would you expect from your nanny?" Karen's tone is firm as her face hardens.

The suddenness of the question throws Greg and me as we stare at one another unsure of what to say next.

"Um... Well..." I turn to Greg for help, who looks back at me dumbstruck. I return to lock eyes with Karen again. "Well, I think that if my kids did something wrong while with a nanny, I would expect the nanny to feed back to us, and we as parents deal with the matter in a way we feel appropriate."

"I disagree. I believe any adult looking after your children should enforce discipline that they see fit."

There's a coldness in Karen's reply that alarms me as I sit upright and pull my shoulders back. I hate to imagine what she'd do to my kids in our absence. Not for me, I decide.

"Alright, thank you for coming, Karen." My words come out more curtly than intended, my ears hurting, and my senses jarred. She doesn't take too kindly to that and tips her head once before departing.

"Ugh," I groan once the door closes behind her. "That was awful. She's not the same person on the CV. Who the hell does she think she is? Maybe she kidnapped the real Karen and came in her place."

Leaning against the door, Greg runs a hand down his

face as his shoulders drop. "Well at least we've spared the kids from having to meet both of them. What a nightmare. They might be good for other families but not a chance in hell of them going near our kids."

A bit defeated, I agree and drag myself to the kitchen to top up my bottle of water. "She was so odd, and I didn't like the way she kept glaring at me. Weirdo."

"Lucy," Greg begins, touching my shoulder. "I know that was tough but try to keep an open mind. We still have one more to meet. Some are bound to be crap."

"I know, I know." I sigh, rubbing my temples and blowing out my cheeks. "It's so hard to find someone who fits what we're looking for."

"Let's see how the last one goes Luce, but if the other two are anything to go by, we might be back to the drawing board."

"Don't say that. I'm not going through this crap again." Greg's words linger in my thoughts as I screw the lid back on my water bottle.

Greg puts an arm round my shoulder and squeezes. "Just one more to go," he says in my ear.

I head upstairs to check on the kids who are blissfully unaware of our recent shenanigans downstairs as they lie on cushions on the floor watching Moana. "Listen, you two." I kneel beside them. "After we finish with the last interview, how about we cuddle up on the sofa and watch a something together? You can even choose?"

Their eyes light up, and the restlessness fades as they exchange excited grins. "Can we watch *Moana again*?" Sarah says pointing at the TV. "I want to watch *Transformers*," Matthew butts in as he squares up to his little sister.

"We'll see how much time we have later. We can watch

one today and the other tomorrow," I say, trying to please them both.

As I'm mentally preparing myself, the doorbell rings. Taking a deep breath, I open the door to find Alice, our last candidate. Her modest attire contrasts with the hair cascading down her shoulders, framing her warm brown eyes. She looks different from the well-presented previous applicants though I can't be certain why.

"Hi, Alice. Please, come in." Trying to hide my fatigue, I usher her inside. I recall her impressive CV, which boasts years of experience and glowing references.

"Please, have a seat," I offer after making her a cuppa. She drops onto the sofa and smiles, her movements gentle and controlled.

"Thank you for inviting me to your home." I watch Alice as she speaks, her tone soothing and considerate.

As Alice talks about her background over the next thirty minutes, I find myself drawn in by her quiet confidence and thoughtful responses. There is something about her vulnerability and honesty which resonates with me.

"Thank you for sharing that." I glance across at Greg, who appears happy. We both feel relaxed around Alice and feel it's right to expand on our meeting. "I'd like to ask the kids to join us if that's okay with you?"

Alice's eyes light up and she pushes herself forward to the edge of her seat in anticipation.

I stand at the bottom of the stairs and call up to the kids. It's a few moments before I see them appear on the landing. "Would you mind popping down for a moment? Daddy and I would like you to meet someone. The kids bounce down the stairs and follow me into the lounge where they head to Greg and plant themselves next to him.

I make a sweeping gesture. "Kids, this is Alice. She's a nanny. Alice, this is Matthew and Sarah."

Alice smiles and studies the kids for a few moments before she introduces herself and strikes up a brief conversation with them. Sarah and Matthew seem somewhat reserved as they sit in the tight space between me and Greg, but they squeeze out a few words in reply to her questions before shrinking further into our sides searching for reassurance. I smile at Sarah, who looks embarrassed each time we glance her way.

"I think that's all we need to cover, and we really appreciate the time you've taken to come along. We'll be in touch."

"Of course, no problem." Alice stands and throws on her coat. "Thank you for seeing me. You have a lovely family and home."

I breathe a sigh of relief as I shut the door behind her. I stare at Greg, who hovers in the doorway to the lounge. A smile spreads across my face. "I think she's the one."

Greg raises a hand. "Not so fast. We need to talk about it this evening, and then sleep on it. It's a big decision, Luce."

Greg's right. I know he is. He's always been the voice of reason for my impulsiveness, but in my mind, Alice is a fit for our family. She's the one I want, and I can't wait to give her the good news.

3
ALICE

As I drive toward the Butler's residence for my first interview as their potential nanny, a blend of enthusiasm and nerves tangle inside my stomach. A warm flush of emotion sweeps over me whenever I think of this golden opportunity. After collecting my thoughts, I park round the corner and take the final steps on foot, letting the familiar, leafy street sink in. It looks idyllic, but I've learned to look beyond appearances. Each step towards their door is a step into a new chapter of my life, one that could change everything.

But I know better than to be charmed by a perfect façade.

"Let's do this," I say, as I ring the doorbell.

The door swings open, and there she stands—Lucy Butler. Her eyes sparkle with excitement, and her blonde hair cascades down her shoulders.

"Hi, Alice. Please, come in," she gushes, extending a slender hand for me to shake.

Stepping into their home feels like stepping into a

show house on a new development. The place is everything I would expect from an upwardly mobile, success-driven couple: large, airy rooms filled with expensive furniture, plush deep sofas in the lounge, and a state-of-the-art kitchen with shiny black marble worktops and gloss white units. It's sickeningly perfect, like the façade Lucy has built round herself.

"Would you like tea or coffee?" Lucy's voice lilts with that irritating enthusiasm that makes me want to rip out her vocal cords.

"Tea would be lovely, thank you." I watch her flit round the kitchen like a hummingbird. As she prepares our drinks, I take mental notes of every detail, every potential weakness round me.

"Here we are." Lucy hands me a steaming cup of tea before guiding me into the lounge where she introduces me to her husband, Greg and the bratlings, Matthew and Sarah. I cast an eye in Greg's direction. He still looks the same.

As we sit down, I launch into my well-rehearsed speech, peppering it with anecdotes. Lucy listens, nodding in all the right places.

"Your experience sounds incredible," she enthuses. "And your references are glowing."

"Thank you." Maintaining my fake smile makes my cheeks ache.

My memories drift—my past a shadowy chapter they know nothing about. I remember those days at the gym café, watching Greg from a distance. He never noticed me, just another face in the crowd, but I noticed everything about him. I'd strategically position myself, back turned, sipping tea, ears tuned to his conversations. Each word, each laugh, an insight into their world, one I'm about to step into. A smile plays on my lips as I recall one conversation in particular. Greg and Lucy remain oblivious to my ruminations. They have no idea how closely our paths have already crossed.

"Lucy's driving me mad," Greg grumbled one evening in particular, downing the last of his coffee. "She wants to go back to work, but we need someone to look after the kids."

"Have you thought about an au pair or a nanny? There's a fair number who come from Oz with a working visa. Bloody fit too," one friend said, wiping his mouth after stuffing his fat face with Millionaire Shortbread.

"Or a childminder?" another chipped in. "Make sure they've got long legs, big boobs, and a fit arse. Then we can come round to yours for coffee instead of drinking this piss water." The conversation continued as Greg's friends roared with laughter.

In that moment, I knew I'd found my way in. I pinned my details to the noticeboard at the gym where Greg couldn't ignore them, and I worked tirelessly with local parents on short-term contracts. I even did several leaflet drops in the area. Every agency knew my name, especially after my stint as a nanny to a local MP desperate to return to the Commons in London.

Lucy's eager expression grounds me back to the present. "Your credentials are impressive," she comments, scanning the list of references I've provided. "Especially your work with the MP. How did you manage that?"

"Right place, right time," I shrug. "I've been really fortunate to work with fantastic families."

"It looks like it," Lucy agrees. "If you can handle the pressure of working for an MP, I'm sure our family will be a breeze."

"Every family is unique, but I'm always up for a challenge." I've perfected smiling politely without giving anything away. It takes every ounce of self-control not to let the darkness inside me seep through. I sit on the edge of a plush sofa, my hands clasped together in my lap as I look at Matthew and Sarah.

Lucy turns to the kids stuck between her and Greg. "Matthew, Sarah, Alice is here to talk about maybe becoming your new nanny, but I'll still be here a few days a week. If I'm working from home, I'll only be upstairs."

"Hi, Matthew," I say, feigning enthusiasm. "And hello, Sarah." I turn to the girl, who stares back, nose crinkled with disdain.

"Hi," she mumbles, barely audible before throwing a hand over her face and burying her head in Lucy's side.

"Tell me," I begin, focusing on the task at hand, "what do you both enjoy doing after school?"

"Football!" Matthew yells, making exaggerated kicking motions with his legs.

"Ah, that's great," I say, smiling at him. "And you, Sarah? How about you? Playing Disney princesses?"

She crosses her arms and looks away, pouting. "Nothing."

"Surely there must be something you like to do?" My voice remains gentle and coaxing, but inside, darkness simmers. It bubbles up until I demand that it abates. How satisfying it would be to give this spoilt little princess a gentle push down the stairs, head-first.

"Sarah, be nice," Lucy scolds, though her tone lacks conviction. "She enjoys dancing and drawing.".

"Those sound lovely," I lie through my teeth. "I'm sure we'll find lots of fun activities to do together."

"Alright, kids." Lucy herds them away. "Let me and Daddy finish our chat with Alice."

Once they're out of sight, I allow a small smile to creep across my face. The interview is going well; I've said the right things and played my part perfectly. The interview closes and they see me out.

As I walk away, the door shutting behind me, I smile.

Mission accomplished.

4

LUCY

THE NEXT MORNING, I get up earlier than usual, probably because of our interview with Alice who seems so perfect for the nanny position. Last night, I tossed and turned in bed and woke a few times with cycling thoughts. Doubts kept popping into my head along with a mental image of my precious babies, followed by a tidal wave of questions. *Am I doing the right thing? Who am I really doing it for, me or them? Will it upset the kids?*

With confusion still crowding my mind, I drag myself out of bed, but my head hurts and my body feels exhausted. Grabbing my phone, I head downstairs to the kitchen and call the agency and wait for thirty minutes before I get the confirmation from the agency that I can call Alice.

"Hello?" Alice answers, her voice soft and steady.

"Hi, Alice. It's Lucy Butler." I try to match her calm tone. "I hear the agency has called to offer you the job as our nanny."

"Yes." There's a hint of delight in her voice. "Thank you, Lucy. That's brilliant."

"Oh, that's fantastic. I know it's cheeky, but can you start this afternoon? Just for a few hours, so the kids can start getting comfortable with this new arrangement. I have to admit, I'm still a little worried about leaving them, but I guess any mum feels the same."

"That sounds a good idea. I think it's important for the children to feel safe and at ease with me before we dive into a regular schedule," she replies.

"Phew. Exactly what I was thinking." I pause for a moment. "Can you make it round two o'clock?"

"Works for me. I'm looking forward to it," Alice confirms.

"Me too. See you then." As I pace the kitchen making breakfast for me and the kids, I smile as I mentally confirm that she's exactly what we need. The afternoon can't come soon enough as I pour hot water into my coffee mug and prepare cereal bowls for the kids, Coco Pops for Matthew, and Weetabix for Sarah. *Everything is falling into place.* I allow myself a moment of pure optimism before diving back into the whirlwind of preparations for Alice's arrival.

"Greg. Kids." I call out, unable to contain my enthusiasm. "Alice said yes. She's starting this afternoon." I hear our bedroom door opening and the sound of Greg coming downstairs, his footsteps heavy, followed seconds behind by lighter footsteps as the kids race to join us.

"Really?" Greg loops his tie under his shirt collar and does his classic Windsor knot. He looks at me with furrowed brows, but a hint of a smile tugs at his lips. "You could have waited for me before calling her. That's great news, love. Alright." My husband takes a deep breath before continuing. "But let's set ground rules for integrating Alice into our home life. For the first few days, she shouldn't be left alone with the kids. That means you'll have to work from home initially, Lucy."

"Are you serious?" At his edict, frustration bubbles through me. I want to get back to my usual routine, but I know Greg is being protective. "Fine, but only for a while." I can feel the heat rising in me, but Greg leans in and kisses me softly, diffusing it almost instantly.

"You'll be fine." He smiles and turns to the children. "And remember, kids, always be on your best behaviour with Alice, right?"

"Okay, Daddy," Sarah replies. Matthew nods. Greg gives each of them a quick hug and kiss before heading out to work, leaving me to manage the chaos that is our morning routine.

The moment Greg's car disappears off the drive, I grab my phone and dial Beth, who sounds out of breath and rushed off her feet. "Beth, you okay?"

"Hiya, Luce. Yeah, I'm good. Trying to change the bedding. Is it me, or do you need to have four very long arms to change a king-size duvet cover? Bloody knackering."

I agree and laugh. "Guess what? Alice is starting today. And my company wants me back on a temp to perm contract as a trial and mainly working remotely for now with the odd day in the office for meetings with suppliers to do reviews of the next season's collection. It's perfect."

"No way. Blimey, you move quick. Luce, that's fantastic. You must be over the moon."

"I am. Finally, it feels like everything's falling into place." As we chat, my gaze wanders through the house, taking in the neatened rooms and the space I've cleared for Alice's arrival.

Later that afternoon, Alice arrives at our doorstep on time. It's bang on two p.m. I'm impressed. Her hair is pulled back into a low ponytail, and her old-fashioned clothes give her an air of modesty that I find reassuring. She smiles, her brown eyes brimming with a quiet confidence that puts me at ease.

"Come in, Alice." I step aside to let her enter. "Let me show you round." We start in the lounge, which she's already familiar with. I point out the cosy reading nook by the window, where the children love to curl up with their books. "Feel free to use any of the toys or games here to keep the kids entertained," I suggest, gesturing to the stacked shelves that line one wall.

"Thank you, Lucy," Alice replies softly.

As we move through the house, I'm struck by how attentive Alice is to every detail. She asks thoughtful questions about the children's routines and preferences, taking care not to miss anything important. It's clear that she cares about her role as a nanny, and I warm to her more and more. "Here's the kitchen again. Help yourself to anything you or the kids might need."

"Thank you," she says.

"This is the playroom," I announce, throwing open the door to a vibrant space filled with colourful toys, games, and craft supplies. "I've stocked it up with everything you'll need to keep the kids engaged and happy."

"Wow, Lucy, I'm impressed. This is amazing." Alice's eyes light up as she takes in the scene.

As Alice steps into the playroom, her gaze lands on Matthew and Sarah huddled together in the corner, their eyes wide with curiosity and apprehension. I watch as Alice approaches and crouches down. "Hello again, you two. What are you both playing?"

"Lego," Matthew replies hesitantly, clutching a half-built spaceship in his hands. Sarah remains silent, as she clings to her brother's arm.

"Would you mind if I join you?" Alice sounds so warm and inviting it almost melts my heart. To my relief, Matthew gives a small nod, and Sarah looks at him for reassurance before mirroring his gesture.

"Here, let me show you how to build a tower." Our new nanny reaches for a handful of Lego bricks. As the three of them work together to construct colourful structures, I hover in the doorway feeling a mixture of hope and concern. But as my children interact with Alice, their nervousness begins to melt away, replaced by genuine enthusiasm and excitement.

"Look, Alice!" Sarah shouts as she proudly holds up her finished tower. "It's taller than yours."

"Wow, Sarah, that's fantastic," Alice replies, "And, Matthew, your spaceship looks amazing. Can I see it up close?"

"Okay." My son hands Alice his creation.

Relief washes over me at the progress we've made in just a few minutes. With every step, I can feel the tension releasing from my body, replaced by a growing confidence that I've made the right decision. Despite Greg's warning, I leave them alone for a short while. It's important for the kids to bond with Alice without me being around. I still make sure that I pop my head around the corner every so often, so they know I'm not far away, and it's not long before I realise that the day has flown by, filled with laughter, stories, and games. But now, as the evening draws near, I pop back into the lounge and hover in the doorway as the kids plead with Alice for one last story before she leaves.

"Please, Alice," Sarah says, her voice a mix of excitement and exhaustion. "Just one more?"

"Alright," she agrees, "but only one, and then it's time for dinner." Alice picks up a worn, well-loved book from the shelf, its spine creaking as it opens. As she reads, Matthew and Sarah lean in closer, hanging on every word.

Greg arrives and I tell him to be quiet as we both wait for Alice to finish before ordering the kids to wash their hands before dinner. Alice places the book back on the shelf and tidies up round her.

"Sounds like you've made quite an impression on the little ones," Greg says, his calm voice betraying a hint of surprise.

"Hello, Mr Butler," she says, "I didn't realise it was so late."

"Greg, please," he says, correcting her. "Lucy told me you had a successful first day with Matthew and Sarah."

"Thank you. It's gone pretty well, I think. I'm glad they enjoyed it," Alice says.

"From what I've seen, you're off to an excellent start." His stern expression softens ever so slightly. "Now, if you'll excuse me, I should go change out of these work clothes."

"Of course." Alice watches as he disappears up the stairs. "I should probably go now. I hope it's been a good experience for you too?" Alice throws on her coat and heads for the front door.

I smile as I follow her, opening the door and standing to one side. "It's been great. I wasn't sure what to expect if I'm honest. But as first days go, I think it's been a roaring success. Thank you so much for agreeing to help our family."

After I close the door, I head up to our bedroom. With his shirt off, my husband looks every inch the man I fell in love with. I come round to face him and slide my hands round his waist. "Greg," I kiss him and smile, "this was the right choice. Alice is amazing with the kids."

My husband stiffens a bit. "Lucy, I'm glad you're happy, but we still need to be careful. We've only met Alice, and she hasn't even been properly alone with the children yet."

"I know, darling," I concede, a hint of frustration seeping into my voice. "But everything went so well today, didn't it? The kids like her already. It can only get better."

"True," Greg agrees, "But there's more to trust than a first impression."

"Gregory Butler," I squeeze his waist, "you're such a worrier sometimes. But I know how you feel, so it's a good thing that I'll be working remotely most of the time to begin with."

As I reassure Greg, I think Alice has come just in time. She's proved herself today, and now I can return to my old job with far less guilt. A spark of optimism flickers inside me. It feels like the universe is granting me a second chance at my career, lightening the weight of emptiness that's been anchoring my heart.

5

ALICE

I press my face into my pillow as screeching screams rip from my throat. Tears soak into my pillowcase as I squeeze my eyelids shut to stop them. So many ragged and choppy breaths shake my chest that I worry my ribcage might explode. The nightmares and flashbacks haunt me every night. I sleep very little, as I'm afraid of what I might see or discover. And yet, there's so much missing. The final pieces of the jigsaw elude me. Regardless of my efforts, I hate to feel like this. I never asked for this, and yet I fear it will never go away.

Lucy Butler will be my saviour.

But the cost of saving my life will be losing her own.

It's the same every time. The flashbacks strike me, vivid and unbidden, as I stand in the silent garden, the scent of freshly cut grass heavy in the air. I'm transported back to a time when I was a little girl, my long hair tied up with a scrunchie, playing with my older brother, Jordan. He's there in the garden with me, bossing me round as he always did, but I adored him.

"Here, put this one on top," Jordan commands,

thrusting a wooden block into my small hands. I obey without questioning him, stacking it atop the teetering tower we've built together.

"Like this, Jordan?" I ask, seeking his approval. My eyes are wide with happiness, my voice soft and innocent.

"Yep." My brother beams down at me. I feel a warmth spread through my chest. Mum watches us from the kitchen window, a proud smile shaping her lips.

"Alright, now let's play hide-and-seek," Jordan suggests, the excitement clear in his tone. "I'll count to twenty and you go hide."

"Okay." I rush off to find a spot towards the end of the garden where overgrown bushes create the perfect hidy-hole. He counts aloud, his voice echoing in the warm air.

As I crouch behind a large bush, my heart races. I peek out from my hiding place, glimpsing Jordan's searching gaze, feeling the thrill of the game and the connection with my beloved brother.

"Ready or not, here I come," he calls out, his voice filled with authority. I stifle a giggle, holding my breath as I watch him scan the area, looking behind the shed and searching along the treeline at the side of our garden.

But as the game wears on, I notice Jordan isn't really trying to find me. Instead, he seems more interested in wasting time and teasing me to make the game last longer, as if toying with me for his amusement. I feel a twinge of unease, but still, I look up to him. He's my big brother, after all.

"Come out, come out, wherever you are," he taunts, grinning. I stay crouched behind the bush, feeling the twigs scratch at my skin, wondering why he's being so mean. But despite the hurt and confusion, I cling to the belief that Jordan must have a reason to act this way.

Maybe it's part of the game I tell myself, trying to rationalise his behaviour.

"Jordan, can't you find me?" I call out, hoping to prompt an end to a long wait. He stops, listening, a small smile playing on his lips that I can't quite decipher.

"Ah, there you are!" Jordan shouts, running over to my hiding place with a victorious smirk. As he pulls me up by the arm, I wince at his tight grip but try not to show it.

"Let's go inside and have something to eat." My brother leads me back towards the house. Eager for a break from his teasing, I nod in agreement, following him.

In the kitchen, our mum has left two generous portions of chocolate cake on the counter. One slice is larger than the other, and as we approach, I see Jordan's eyes dart between them before fixing on the bigger piece.

"Let's play another game," he says, his tone mischievous. "Rock, paper, scissors. Winner gets the bigger slice."

Before I can even process what he's saying, Jordan throws out a rock while my hand forms scissors. He grins, claiming the larger portion for himself. The feeling of unease grows within me, but I stay silent, not wanting to cause a fuss.

"Maybe next time," he mocks, taking a large bite of his cake and smirking at me as crumbs fall onto his plate. "And you better hurry and eat your bit or I'll have that too." A familiar tension builds in the air. I take smaller and quicker bites of mine, trying to ignore the sting of his words.

"You know," he licks a dollop of chocolate icing off his fork, "I've always wondered how someone so slow at hide-and-seek could be so good at eating cake."

"Jordan, please stop." A sadness washes over me—an uncomfortable cocktail of hurt and anger.

"Aw, poor you," he scoffs, rolling his eyes. "Can't handle a little joke?"

His taunting continues, each remark more hurtful than the last. My shoulders shake as I fight back tears, my slice of cake forgotten on the plate in front of me. I want to shout at him, to tell him how much his words upset me. I want to know why he's being so horrible all the time, but something holds me back. The fear of making things even worse.

"Stop it, Jordan," I finally say, my voice shaking with anger as I slap my fork onto the table and fold my arms across my chest. But instead of feeling bad, a twisted satisfaction lingers in his eyes as if he's enjoying the power he holds over me.

"Or what?" he challenges, leaning closer, daring me to defy him. "You'll cry like a baby?"

I stare at him. I don't understand why he's doing this; after all, we used to be inseparable.

"Are you really that stupid?" Jordan sneers, watching me with an infuriating smirk. "Sometimes I wonder if you'll ever grow up."

"Leave her alone, Jordan," Mum says from the doorway, her hands resting on her hips. She looks stern, but I can see the worry in her eyes as she takes in my tearful expression.

"Relax, Mum," Jordan says, the picture of innocence. "We're only having a bit of fun, aren't we?"

I swallow back the lump in my throat and force a nod. I don't want Mum to worry about me, even though I'm desperate for the teasing to stop.

"Fine," Mum warns, unconvinced. "But if I hear any more unkind words to your sister, you'll go straight to your room and go to bed without dinner."

"Okay, Mum." Despite my brother's charming smile, I

know what he's thinking as she reluctantly leaves the room.

As soon as she's gone, Jordan glares at me. "You're pathetic," he hisses, leaning towards me. "Always hoping Mummy sticks up for you."

"Jordan, please." Tears prick at the corners of my eyes. I try to hold on to the memories of us playing together, laughing and sharing secrets, but they seem so distant now, replaced by this ever-present new version of my brother who only seems to enjoy hurting me.

"Aw, are you going to cry?" Jordan mocks.

My vision blurs as the tears finally spill over, and I wipe them away with the backs of my hands, hating myself for showing him how much his words affect me. But even as I cry, I wonder what happened to the brother I once adored and why he's become so cruel.

"Enough!" Mum shouts from the doorway, her face flushed with anger. "Jordan, you're grounded for a week. Go to your room."

"Come on, Mum," Jordan pleads, that same charming smile appearing on his lips. "I was only joking. Can't she take a joke?"

"Apologise to your sister," Mum demands, not falling for his act this time.

"Sorry." Despite the platitude, Jordan's voice drips with insincerity. But Mum seems satisfied for now, and she leaves us once again.

My heart jumps as I watch the malicious glint in Jordan's eyes. He steps closer, his voice low and threatening. "Listen, you better keep quiet about this. Or else I'll tell all your friends that you still wet the bed."

A mixture of rage and fear swirls inside me. "Go on then," I spit out, my voice trembling. "Tell them whatever you want. You're so mean and horrible."

"Fine, have it your way." He sneers, clearly not expecting my defiance. With one last glare, he turns on his heel and storms away from our garden, heading towards the street.

I can't let him get away with this. Not again. My anger fuels me as I race after him, chasing him into our street lined with trees and well-manicured lawns. Each step feels like an act of rebellion, a refusal to cower before my brother any longer.

"Jordan!" I shout, my voice echoing down the street.

But Jordan doesn't respond. He keeps running, his back to me as if I'm nothing more than an annoying fly buzzing round him. As I chase after him, my chest tightens, and I can't catch my breath. But I refuse to give up.

"Jordan, stop!" My voice cracks with desperation. "Please, talk to me. I don't understand why you're being like this."

Briefly, he appears to hesitate, a flicker of vulnerability in his stride. But he shakes it off and continues running.

"Jordan!" I scream after him, tears streaming down my face. "Why are you doing this?"

But still, he doesn't answer as the distance between us grows.

My heart pounds in my chest as I chase after Jordan, the ache in my legs growing stronger with each step. The familiar sight of our quiet, tree-lined street blurs round me as I focus on my brother's retreating figure.

"Jordan, stop." My voice is raw from shouting. "You can't run away from this forever."

He doesn't even glance back at me, his determination to escape unwavering.

"Please," I beg. "I want to understand what happened to you."

But my words seem to fall on deaf ears. As Jordan

rounds a corner, I force my weary legs to keep moving, refusing to let him slip away without a fight.

"Jordan, please." A choked sob escapes my lips. Suddenly, the sound of screeching tyres fills the air, sending a jolt of panic through me. I gasp as I round the corner, only to see Jordan frozen in place, his face a mask of terror.

"Jordan, watch out!" I scream, my heart in my mouth as terror takes hold of my body.

The car veers off course with a violent jerk, a menacing hulk of metal out of control. Time splits, turning into fragments, each second stretching longer than the last. Jordan's scream pierces the chaos, a sound that etches itself into my memory. I stand rooted to the spot, my own scream trapped in my lungs.

After one strangled heartbeat, an eerie silence descends like a suffocating blanket. My ears ring. The world momentarily muted. The click of a car door breaks the quiet, followed by the sharp click of heels against the tarmac. I barely register the woman rushing towards me, her faced etched with shock. Her touch barely registers through my numbness as she wraps a warm arm around my shoulder.

Lucy Butler's arm.

6

LUCY

IT'S ONLY BEEN a few days since Alice joined us, and already she's become an integral part of the Butler household. It's as if she's always been here, slipping into our lives like a missing puzzle piece.

"Come on, you two." Alice claps her hands together as she leads the children through a series of creative exercises. Her enthusiasm is infectious, and the kids are loving it. She's attentive and gentle, yet firm when needed. Perhaps I'm a tad envious because there are times the kids completely ignore me.

With Alice, they hang on every word with rapt attention. Their ability to so easily forget our former dynamic breaks my heart.

The day continues in a whirlwind of activity. Alice helps me round the house, folding laundry and tidying up without a fuss. We share brief moments of conversation, and despite the age difference, we get on well.

"Lucy, would you like a cuppa? I'm making myself one," Alice asks.

"Please," I reply, as I unload the dishwasher.

As Alice busies herself with the kettle, I reflect on the way she interacts with Greg and the kids. It's as if she's known them forever. I feel a pang of jealousy mixed with admiration. How does she do it? But then I realise I know so little about her. Nothing about her past, family, dreams, or aspirations.

"Here you are." She hands me a steaming mug of tea.

"Thanks for all your help today," I say.

"It's my pleasure."

As we stand in the kitchen, a comfortable silence surrounds us. I cradle my mug in both hands. "I never asked, but are you from around Cambridge?"

Alice lifts her mug and pauses. "Erm, no. I've moved round a bit but mostly worked in London and the South East."

Not what I asked, but I continue to be nosey. "So where are your family from?" I wait and it's a while before Alice replies, which I find odd.

"Sudbury, Suffolk. Well, close to it."

"Ah, I know it. I've been round that area a few times over the years for work. Suffolk is lovely," I say.

"It is," Alice replies.

"And are your family still there? Parents?"

Alice nods. "My parents still live there but I don't have any contact with them anymore." She sets her mug down on the counter. "I'm going to check on Matthew and Sarah."

As I raise my brow, I find her response a bit odd. I wonder why Alice cut the conversation off and left so sharply. Perhaps she doesn't get on with her parents, hence the reason for the brief replies. It would explain why she's moved round for jobs so much. Anything than going back home.

I shake off the curiosity for now and focus on

preparing dinner. A simple pasta and sauce this evening, with home-made garlic bread. I glance over towards the lounge at Alice, who's helping Matthew and Sarah with a puzzle.

As I drain the pasta and mix it into the sauce, the front door clicks open. Greg strides through the door, his briefcase in hand and wearing that same serious expression he always has after work. His eyes scan the lounge, taking in the sight of Alice and the children before landing on me.

"Evening, everyone." He hangs up his coat and loosens his tie. The kids cheerfully greet him, their excitement contagious as they abandon the puzzle to give their dad a hug.

"Hey," I call out, plating up the pasta. "Dinner's about ready."

"Excellent timing, Luce." My husband returns my smile as he comes in and plants a kiss on my cheek before heading towards the dining table. The kids race in seconds later and scramble to pull out their chairs in readiness.

"Alice, are you joining us?" I ask.

"Erm, I was going to leave you in peace," she says.

"Oh, please stay. Mummy, can Alice stay for dinner?" Sarah pleads, her eyes wide and hopeful.

"Of course she can. She's always welcome. Alice?"

Alice hesitates in the doorway before accepting and taking the spare seat beside Greg.

"Thank you," Alice murmurs, shifting in her chair.

"Right, let's eat." I take my seat opposite Greg as we all tuck into the meal. We chat about our day, sharing stories, and for a moment, everything feels normal. Alice fits seamlessly into the conversation, attentive and considerate, making us feel like she has always been a part of our lives.

"Tell us about your day, Alice," Greg suggests, his voice measured but inviting. He forks more pasta into his mouth and nods appreciatively.

Alice hesitates for a moment. "Well, we had a lovely time playing hide-and-seek in the garden. We worked on placing words into sentences, and Sarah helped me make chocolate cookies for everyone."

"Thank you, Alice. They were delicious." They went down a treat with my coffee.

"I hope you left some for Daddy." Greg glances across towards Sarah.

"There's *one* left for you." Sarah giggles.

"Did anything interesting happen at work today, Greg?" Alice asks, turning to him.

Greg pauses, considering his answer. "There was a disagreement between two departments, but we sorted it in the end." He keeps the details vague as if to shield Alice from the mundane reality of office politics.

"Sounds difficult," Alice sympathises, her brow furrowing in concern. "You must be tired after such a long day."

"Nothing I can't handle," Greg assures her. Despite his calm exterior, I know the stress he keeps bottled up inside him, the pressure that builds until it threatens to explode.

"Lucy," Alice's gaze rests on me now, "how was *your* day?"

"Busy, as always," I admit. "But having you here has been a godsend. I feel like I can breathe again."

"Greg, do you have any big plans for the weekend?" Alice asks, her eyes still on him.

"Nothing too exciting." My husband is a master at keeping his deep voice measured and calm. "I'm catching up on paperwork and spending time with the family."

"Sounds perfect to me," Alice says.

The Perfect Nanny

As I study their interaction, I'm hit with a jolt of surprise. Despite her quiet nature, she draws Greg out of his shell like so few others can.

With the meal drawing to a close, I reflect on how much easier life has become since Alice came into the picture. The children adore her, and even Greg seems to have warmed to her presence. Finally, I feel like we are on the right track.

"Let me help you clear the table," Alice offers, rising from her chair and gathering plates.

After playing with the kids for a short while, Greg disappears off to the study. Alice stops by the table, her eyes lingering on the children's faces for a moment. "I should go now," she says before saying goodbye to me and heading off.

Watching Alice effortlessly clear the table and bring warmth into our home, I feel hopeful. Life is already getting easier, and I look forward to what the future holds as we all get to know each other even better.

7

ALICE

Week after week, I weave myself deeper into the fabric of their lives, an insidious thread in the tapestry of the Butler family. My bond with the children, a surprising development, creeps up on me. Perhaps it's a flicker of maternal instinct, but it really doesn't matter why. To me, Matthew and Sarah are mere chess pieces in a game with high stakes, a game where the end justifies the means. They're destined for a fractured future, collateral damage in a war they didn't choose. Their mother will fast become a fragile shadow of the uppity, entitled bitch she once was as she teeters on the brink of her own sanity, oblivious to the puppet strings I hold.

With my mission clear, my resolve proves unyielding. I must maintain this façade, the perfect nanny, the saviour in the Butlers' increasingly chaotic world. They lean on me, their trust growing, without the foggiest notion that I'm the architect of their downfall. In this house of cards, I'm a silent storm, waiting to unleash my own special brand of karma. For Lucy, the nightmare has only begun, and even though I'm cloaked in kindness, I'm its harbinger.

Since it's Saturday, Greg and Lucy head off for a cosy breakfast and then a trip into town to do some shopping. So, I've taken Matthew and Sarah out for a few hours so they can burn off their never-ending energy. We've fed the ducks and now I watch as they race from one playground activity to another.

Matthew and Sarah have grown fond of me, and they trust me, which is exactly what I need. Due to the mild weather, the park is busy. With only a few clouds in the sky, and a light breeze, kids ride round on bikes, a few joggers pound the paths round the pond, and families walk their dogs along a trail. Idyllic bliss for some, I guess. For me, it gives me time to think, but that's where the problem lies. The more I think, the angrier I get. I'm not like normal people. Sitting on the bench, I can't appreciate the joys of life, plan for my next holiday, or wonder where my next boyfriend will come from. I'm obsessive. When I get an idea in my head, that's all I think of. I'm my worst enemy because the more I obsess, the more fuel I throw on the fire that rages inside of me.

"Hi there, Alice." The voice of Lucy's friend, Beth, breaks through my thoughts and makes me jump, drawing my attention to her approaching figure.

"Hello, Beth." I greet her with a soft smile, as her dog excitedly runs round her feet. "Sorry, I was miles away for a second."

Beth laughs. "Don't worry, I'm like that all the time. I'm sure I invented the word 'airhead'. How are you settling into your new role as a nanny?"

"Quite well, thank you." I watch Matthew and Sarah playing on the swings. "I've always loved caring for children, and those two are a joy to look after. Besides, it pays the bills and gives me a sense of purpose," I joke. "How's Alfie?" I stroke her cockapoo, who's now rubbing against my legs. "I'd love to have a dog. They're great company." I try to maintain my façade of innocence. "But my mum never allowed it. She thought having another mouth to feed would be too much of a burden."

Beth nods in agreement, her eyes drifting to her dog. "I know what you mean. I've always wanted a dog, and now that I have one, I can't imagine life without him. Your mum sounds quite strict." Her brow furrows. "What was it like growing up?"

I prepare to weave the web of lies I've crafted, knowing they'll get back to Lucy. "It was difficult," I begin, my voice trembling enough to appear genuine as I gaze at the ground for a moment. "My dad left when I was young. He liked the company of a bottle of Scotch, and I never had a father figure in my life." In reality, my upbringing was far from troubled. My parents were kind and loving, and my brother was my best friend. But Beth doesn't need to know that.

"Ah, Alice, I'm so sorry," Beth says, her voice full of sympathy. "That must have been really hard for you."

I muster a feeble smile. "It was, but I've learnt to accept it and move on."

Beth places a comforting hand on my shoulder. "Well, if you ever need someone to talk to, reach out. I'm always here for you. I'm a good listener, promise."

"Thanks, Beth." A sick satisfaction washes over me at how easily she falls for my lies. "I appreciate that."

"Of course. I must head back, so I'll catch you another time." She gives me another warm smile before continuing her dog walk.

As Beth disappears, I glance back at Matthew and Sarah, still playing close by. For now, they trust me, and that's all I need. As I watch them play, their laughter echoes through the air. I keep a close eye on them, ensuring their safety while maintaining my control. The power I have over them is intoxicating, like a drug coursing through my veins. As much as I feel apathetic towards the children, there's something thrilling about having such influence over their lives.

A tall chubby boy near the slide draws my attention, his snide expression unmistakable as he teases Matthew, blocking him from climbing up. I feel my chest tighten, and the darkness within me stirs.

I rise from the bench and stroll over to the two boys. With each step, my pulse quickens as my hands curl into fists. "Sarah, why don't you head over to the swing for a second, sweetie? I'll come and push you shortly." Sarah doesn't question me at all and playfully skips to the swings a few feet away. I turn towards the porky little bastard. "Having fun, are we?" I ask as I approach him. He turns to me with a defiant smirk, not expecting me to do much. But that smirk soon fades when he meets my icy stare. "Listen carefully." I lean in so only he can hear me, I point my finger. "Do you see the big pond over there?" Porky glances over before returning to meet my eyes. "Well, if you don't stop teasing my boy right now, I'll drag you over there, throw you in, and hold your head under the water until you choke to death, you little fat shit. Do you understand?"

The boy's eyes widen in terror, and his face drains of colour. Without a word, he scuttles away, running straight into the arms of his mother. She's been watching from a distance and must have seen the fear spreading on her son's face.

"Did you just threaten my child?" she demands, striding over, her voice shrill and accusatory.

"Your child was bullying mine." I quickly mask the storm of emotions churning inside me. "I only reminded him of the consequences of his actions."

"Who the hell do you think you are?" she hisses, her face contorted with rage.

I could point out she looks like the poster girl for McDonald's and KFC, judging from her waddling bulk, but I hold back with my thoughts. "Someone who will protect these children at all costs." My gaze travels her substantial bulk. Then I lock eyes with her and stare her down. "If that means making sure your son learns a lesson, then so be it. Trouble starts at home, right?"

"Don't you dare talk to me like that. Right, I'm calling the police," Porky's mum rants as she plunges her hand into her pocket to retrieve her phone.

I don't give her the chance to even dial the first nine, grabbing her phone and throwing it on the grass beyond the fence surrounding the playground. That will give her time to cool off as she hunts for it… and burn some of those extra calories before the button on her jeans pops open. With that, I turn away, walking back to Matthew and Sarah. Their innocent smiles warm my heart, but deep down, the darkness remains, always waiting for its next opportunity to surface.

8

LUCY

THE WEEKEND SEEMS like an age ago as I head back from my office. Navigating the winding roads back home after one of those rare in-person meetings, I notice the car doesn't sound right. Working remotely has helped me ease back into the rhythm of work, but I'm still getting to grips with the face-to-face malarkey. My fingers tighten round the steering wheel, my eyes flicking between the road ahead and the dashboard, praying I don't break down. There are no warning lights on the dash, but then again, if any popped on, I doubt I'd know their meaning. But the lumpy drive doesn't feel right, so I pull over onto the verge, and leave my hazards flashing.

I swing the door open, making sure it's safe for me to walk round the car without being run over by a lorry and search for anything that looks odd. The tyres look fine and the exhaust isn't hanging off, so that's a good start. Nothing obvious leaps out at me, so with a shake of my head I climb back behind the wheel. "Probably just my imagination," I tell myself, forcing a laugh. The car springs to life, and I continue my journey knowing I'm not far away, and besides I have breakdown cover.

Pulling into our driveway, I note Alice waiting at the door. She offers a tentative smile as she opens it, her brown eyes warm and welcoming.

"Hi, Lucy. How was your meeting?" Her voice is soft.

"Exhausting," I sigh, retrieving my bag from the passenger seat. That's when I notice it—the slow hiss of air escaping from the front tyre. "Bloody hell." With a groan, I slam the car door with more force than intended.

"Is everything alright?" Alice steps closer, peering at the tyre.

"Seems I've got a slow puncture. I must have hit a pothole or picked up a nail," I explain. "Just what I need after a long day."

"Do you want me to call someone?"

"No, no. Greg can sort it later." I force a smile, unwilling to let this ruin my evening. "Thanks, though. Let's get inside. I need a drink. I'm knackered."

"Of course." Alice steps aside as I enter the house.

"Hey, kids," I call out, my voice full of enthusiasm despite my fatigue. "Mummy's home."

"Hi, Mummy!" my children shout back, popping their heads out from the lounge.

As I join them, a broken lamp on the floor behind the door catches my eye and I grind to a halt. Toys lay scattered round it. "What happened here?"

The room falls silent. Neither Matthew nor Sarah seem eager to take responsibility for the mess.

"Did either of you break this?" I question again, my eyes scanning each of my children's faces, searching for a hint of guilt.

"Wasn't me," one mutters, while the other shakes their head.

I sigh, feeling the burden of the day settling on my shoulders. It's then that Alice steps forward, her hands wringing together.

"Lucy, I'm so sorry. I must have knocked it over by accident earlier when we were playing," she apologises, her eyes filled with genuine remorse.

"Thank you for owning up, Alice. But please be more careful in the future. This cost a small fortune."

"Of course, Lucy. I promise you, it won't happen again."

"Alright, let's clean this up and move on." I walk out and head to the kitchen.

I pour myself a glass of red wine, hoping it will help calm my frazzled nerves. As I take a sip, my eyes wander to the back window above the sink, and I narrow my gaze. I notice the garden gate ajar. My breath catches as I also spot a flowerpot tipped over on the ground, dirt spilling out onto the patio.

"Did any of you go outside today? The back gate is open, and the flowerpot has been knocked over!" I ask the children.

"No, Mum," they reply in unison, their expressions puzzled as they come in, followed by Alice.

"Let me check," Alice interrupts, her concern clear as she walks towards the back door. "We were at the park all morning, and when we got back I don't remember seeing the garden gate open."

A chill travels down my back as I attempt to piece together what could've happened. What if someone tried to break in? "That's odd. Did you see anyone lurking round this morning?" I check the back door is locked, even though Alice checked moments ago.

"No. Nothing," she replies.

The kids exchange uneasy glances, sensing my rising

panic. Before I can say anything else, Greg's car pulls into the driveway. He steps inside, his brow furrowed as he registers the chaotic scene before him.

"Everything okay here?" he asks.

"No. Someone left the garden gate wide open, or someone tried to break in." I gesture towards the unlocked gate and toppled flowerpot.

"Ah." Greg rubs the back of his neck. "That... might've been me. I took out the rubbish this morning and probably forgot to lock it again after going to the garage. I can't remember, but I thought I'd shut it."

"Greg, Jesus, you have to be more careful. We can't afford to be so careless about our safety. Anything could have happened. You gave a burglar an open invitation to break into our home."

"I know, Lucy. I'm sorry," he replies. "I'll be more careful. I was in a hurry I guess. I'll lock it now."

But even as I nod, there is something is amiss. Unsettled, I glance towards the garden gate once more and think that we were lucky this time. I think back to four weeks ago when neighbours six doors down were burgled when out shopping. The burglars got in through the rear patio doors and police dropped leaflets at all the houses asking us to be vigilant. The unease gnaws at me, like an itch I can't quite reach. My gaze keeps drifting back to the garden gate, now locked but still taunting me. Greg wraps his arm round my shoulders, pulling me in for a comforting hug.

"Lucy, love, don't worry so much," he says gently. "We all make mistakes, and luckily nothing happened."

"I know," I reply, trying to sound convinced. "It's just... everything seems off today."

"Life gets hectic sometimes." Greg squeezes me reassuringly. "But look at how well Alice has been handling the kids. They're better behaved than ever."

I nod in agreement. I can't deny that. Our home, usually a whirlwind of chaos, has become calmer under Alice's watchful eye. She's been a godsend, her presence soothing even the most frayed nerves.

"Alright," I concede, forcing a small smile. "You're right. I'm overthinking things."

"Exactly," Greg agrees, pressing a gentle kiss to my forehead. "Now, why don't you go relax while I rustle up dinner?"

"Okay." I allow myself to be led towards the lounge.

As I sink into the plush cushions of the sofa, I come up with a new mantra, repeating it like a lifeline. *Everything is fine. Everything is fine.* "Normal, hectic family life."

Closing my eyes, I inhale the familiar scent of our home. For a moment, I almost believe it.

9

LUCY

"Come on, Sarah, put your shoes on. We're going to Granny and Grandad's," Greg says, as he places their breakfast bowls in the dishwasher. Sarah fumbles with her trainers, so Greg kneels and helps, while Matthew wiggles his feet into his trainers and stomps round in them, too lazy to undo the laces. I watch from the doorway as Greg helps Sarah into her coat, while Matthew fidgets beside them.

"Bye, Mummy," Sarah calls out, waving to me.

"Bye, sweetheart. Have fun at Granny's." I wave back, blowing her a kiss, trying to hide the exhaustion in my voice.

"See you later, Luce. Get some work done, okay?" Greg says before ushering the kids out of the door.

"Bye, love." I wave them off, then I check the time on my phone. I've got a few hours to nip to the shops and post office before my work Zoom call. It'll be nice to have a bit of peace for once.

As their car disappears round the corner, an eerie silence falls over the empty house. My mind feels frazzled.

Staying at home looking after the kids has left me exhausted, frustrated, and a hermit. Even though Alice is helping now, I'm still struggling with stress and fatigue.

"Surely all mums with young children feel tired and stressed?" I mutter to myself, pacing round the lounge. "No need to see a doctor... right?"

I shake off the thought, focusing on what I need to do in the few hours as I grab my purse and head out to run my errands.

In the brief sanctuary of my car, I let out a long breath, the familiar streets blurring past. Post Office ticked off my list. I cling to the normality of errands, a temporary shield against the relentless tide of stress and doubts. But as I pull into the driveway, that fragile peace shatters, that recurrent sense of unease creeping in.

I return from the shops and place my bag on the dining table. There's a slight draft coming from the back of the kitchen, and I stop in my tracks as my eyes are drawn to the back door, which is ajar. My pulse quickens, and a sinking feeling sets in. Did I leave it open? I'm certain that I locked it before leaving.

Unable to shake the unease creeping into my chest, I step towards it cautiously, my heart pounding in my ears. "Hello?" I call out, as though expecting an answer. Silence greets me, only heightening my anxiety. *Did someone break in?* But nothing appears to be disturbed in the kitchen. The drawers are closed, the pile of letters still sits in a heap on the table, including the tenner that Greg left beside it. But I need to search the house to be sure.

I start with the lounge, scanning every corner and nothing seems out of place, but I can't stop the incessant whisper in my mind. As I move through the house, silence follows me. Everything appears to be intact, and nothing is missing. The bedrooms are the same, no signs of disturbance either. The children's toys are scattered on their bedroom floors as usual, while our bedroom looks untouched. I check under the beds and in the wardrobes, my rapid breathing doing little to calm me. *Nothing... nothing odd*, I try to reassure myself. But the unease doesn't leave, lingering and sending an icy shiver snaking up my spine.

In my panic, I dial Greg's number. The phone rings once, twice, before he answers.

"Lucy?"

"Greg," I gasp, trying to steady my breathing, "Can you come home? Now."

"Alright, what happened?"

"I found the kitchen door open when I got back from the shops. I can't get rid of the suspicion that someone was here."

"Stay put, Lucy. I'll leave Mum and Dad's right away and be there as soon as I can."

"Please hurry," I say, hanging up. I sink onto the couch, my heart still racing, the silence of the empty house amplifying every creak and groan.

It feels like an eternity before I hear the familiar sound of Greg's car pulling into the driveway. The front door clicks open, and Greg strides in, his tall frame filling the doorway. He wastes no time, scanning the room with a furrowed brow.

"Lucy, are you alright?"

"I'm scared," I admit, my voice cracking.

"Let me check the house and garden."

I watch as Greg moves through each room, doing the same thing I already did, examining every nook and cranny, before venturing outside into the garden. He scans the garden before inspecting the bushes, back gate and even the shed, with a hawk-like gaze.

As he returns, I can see the frustration clouding his features. "There's nothing, Lucy. No signs of forced entry or disturbance. No footprints or anything."

"Then what about calling the police?"

"Alright." My husband sighs, looking at me with concern. "I'll call them to be on the safe side. But there's not much they'll be able to do."

"Greg, all the windows are locked. I didn't leave that door open."

"Lucy, you've been frazzled lately; you might have forgotten to lock it like I did with the back gate after I took out the rubbish."

"I didn't forget." My voice rises as anger bubbles inside me.

"Alright, alright." He holds up his hands defensively. "But there's no evidence anyone was here. Maybe it's just one of those things."

"Greg, someone was in our house while I was out. I know it," I insist.

"Lucy, listen to yourself. You have been stressed, and when you are stressed, you can be forgetful." His voice takes on a patronising tone, causing my blood to boil further. "Remember last year when you lost your car at Bluewater, and it took us an hour to find it? Or a few months ago when you left your purse at a Tesco's till?"

My cheeks flush with embarrassment and anger. Why does he have to bring up my past mistakes now? "That's different, Greg. This isn't me being forgetful."

"Or what about that time you left the gas ring alight on the stove *all night*?" He presses on. "When you get stressed, you forget things, Lucy. We both know that."

My nostrils flare. "Stop it. This isn't about me making mistakes. I'm telling you; someone was in our house."

"Lucy, without proof, I can't blindly accept that as fact."

His words cut deep, and I find myself at a loss for words.

"Fine," I finally say, choking back tears. "But I know what I saw."

"Okay, Lucy," he concedes, his voice softening slightly. "I know you think you locked the door, but everything inside is as it should be. All we can do is note any further strange occurrences."

As Greg leaves the kitchen to put on a video for the kids, I'm left alone with my thoughts. My teeth grind in frustration. When my husband gaslights and patronizes me, it raises my hackles.

The silence that follows Greg's return to the kitchen is suffocating, and I grip the edge of the kitchen counter to steady my frustration. "You think I'm losing it again, don't you?" I ask, unable to look him in the eye.

"Lucy." His voice is heavy with concern. "I didn't say that. But I think you haven't been yourself for a long time. Maybe you should talk to someone about this."

"Like who?" I shout, my anger flaring. "A doctor again? A shrink again? So they can tell me I'm another stressed-out mum who can't cope?"

"Remember when Sarah was born?" Greg asks softly, his gaze exploring mine for understanding. "You struggled back then, too. Postnatal depression, wanting to hide away in our bedroom all day feeling overwhelmed... It took you months to bond with her properly. And ever since then, it hasn't taken much to tip you over the edge and find everything too much. Christmas dinner, packing for holidays, stuck in traffic jams on the M11. They have all led to mini meltdowns and outbursts."

The blood drains from my face as memories flood

back. The exhaustion, endless tears, and the crippling sense of failure. The time I left Sarah in her car seat, forgotten for twenty agonising minutes while she slept blissfully unaware. My chest tightens at the thought as a surge of guilt washes over me.

"Please." My voice cracks. My husband's reckless words, dripping with condescension, slice through me, reigniting old wounds with the precision of a surgeon's scalpel—leaving me raw and exposed, a tangle of past pain and present indignation. "Don't remind me of that."

He tilts his head to the side as he regards me much like an exhibit at the zoo. "Lucy, I'm not trying to upset you. I want you to consider that perhaps you're going through something similar now. You've been under a lot of stress lately, and it might be affecting your judgement."

"Or maybe," I fire back, "someone did break into our house, and you're refusing to see it because you'd rather believe I'm losing my mind."

"Please, let's not fight about this," Greg pleads, running a hand through his hair in frustration. "I'm only suggesting that you talk to someone again, just in case. It's not a bad thing to ask for help."

"Fine." Anger bubbles to the surface, threatening to overflow and burn everything in its path like molten lava. "You want me to talk to someone? I will. But if I was right all along, and someone broke into our house... Will you believe me then?"

"Of course I bloody well will, Lucy."

"Right," I mutter, still unconvinced. As Greg leaves the kitchen, I stare at the door through which he disappeared, feeling the weight of his words settling on my shoulders. Is he right? Am I losing myself to stress and fatigue again? The sting of tears prickles my eyes, blurring my vision as echoes of Greg's words linger in my mind. I hate it when he brings up the past, when he uses my own failures against me. I lean against the kitchen counter, my thoughts racing. Perhaps he's right; maybe I need help. But the thought of admitting that I'm not coping well sends a shudder down my spine.

More doubt creeps in. Is it possible that I did leave the door unlocked? But no, I couldn't have. I remember locking it before leaving for the shops. Or was that yesterday? No, it was today. The certainty of that memory steadies me.

10

ALICE

I STAND HIDDEN within the shadows of the trees, my body twitching and keen to get on. I watch as Lucy hurries to her car, checking the contents of her handbag, no doubt making sure she has everything, before flicking her head, her hair bouncing across her shoulders. She's always so animated, even when flustered, a stark contrast to my own reserved nature. She waves to Mr Roberts across the street. A seventy-four-year-old widower who never smiles, hates kids, noise, and litter, and is forever moaning about how the neighbourhood has changed in the twenty-four years he's been living here.

He's far too much of a nosey neighbour for my liking. I've seen his net curtains twitching on so many occasions. It's like he lives by his window. Mind you, with his wife dead now for three years, what else has he got to fill his life? I never see him leave the street but he's always lurking round it or in the woods behind the houses, a one-man neighbourhood watch who wants to know what everyone is doing and who are they doing it with. I've seen him clock me many times, so I've had to be extra careful today and stay out of sight.

"Come on, Lucy. Get on with it. Drive off will you," I murmur, gripping the spare key in my hand.

As soon as the car disappears, I slip from my hiding spot and make my way round to the back of the house. I get up on my toes and reach over the top of the garden gate to unlock it.

Pausing at the back door, I remove my shoes and leave them behind, a precaution to avoid leaving any footprints. I unlock the door to enter the kitchen. After taking a cautious step inside, the familiar scent of their Jo Malone and The White Company fragrant candles fill my nostrils. It's intoxicating and repulsive all at once. I feel out of place in this perfect world. Even though I've been here for a few weeks now, it still feels odd.

Tiptoeing, I make my way through to the front of the house. The lounge is a testament to their picture-perfect life. Cosy, tastefully decorated with the best furniture, and filled with love, or so it seems. But I know better. Their lives are nothing but a façade, and I'm here to tear it apart.

My gaze falls on the alcove, where family photos sit proudly on a shelf. Each frame captures Lucy, Greg, and their children. Each one sickens me further. A sea of smiling faces. Family embraces. Warm, sunny holidays. A Christmas tree and piles of presents with the Butlers posing in front of them. Their happiness feels like a mockery, a cruel reminder of what they've taken from me.

"Disgusting," I mutter as resentment boils inside me. My eyes linger on one particular photograph. Lucy and Greg on their wedding day, beaming with joy. My fingers itch to shatter the glass as I reach out and grab the frame, my hand shaking, desperate to destroy that moment forever, but I stop myself and release my grip.

The Perfect Nanny 69

I press my thumb down over her beautiful face. "Your perfect little world is about to crumble, Lucy. You'll see."

The sound of my heartbeat fills my ears, a relentless drumming that accompanies each step I take deeper into their home. For years, I've lived in their shadow, consumed by feelings of inadequacy and bitterness. Now the tables will turn. It's time for Lucy to feel what it's like to have everything she holds dear snatched away from her.

I head for the larder, my hands trembling from the adrenaline coursing through my veins. The small open bottle of red wine I'd spotted earlier catches my eye. I know it's Lucy who drinks red, as Greg only drinks white wine. Unscrewing the lid, I retrieve a small bottle of zopiclone from my back pocket and pour some of the crushed powder into the wine before giving it a shake. I hate resorting to this medication, but my insomnia has left me with little choice. Sleep is a luxury that has eluded me for many years and though I used to take it, I've resisted the urge recently.

"Sleep tight, Lucy," I murmur, knowing that adding zopiclone to her wine will cause her the same side effects I've endured. I breathe a sigh of satisfaction at the thought of her experiencing the same depression, forgetfulness, hallucinations, and delusions that haunt me during my darkest moments.

With that task done, I head to Lucy's bedroom. As I rummage through her drawers, I feel a twisted sense of satisfaction from violating her personal space. A wicked smile crosses my lips as I find a vibrator in her bedside drawer. Then I snort. Why on earth would she need one when she has the fit Greg in bed beside her every night? *This will do nicely.* I place it into Greg's drawer, hoping it will only add to her confusion.

My twisted games aren't over yet as I pull out a pack of condoms from my back pocket. With a sly grin, I slip one condom into the back pocket of Greg's jeans in the laundry basket, knowing full well that Lucy checks all the pockets before washing them. "Let's see how you feel about this. Enjoy your perfect life while it lasts, Lucy," I say, allowing myself a moment to revel in what I have set in motion.

I thumb through the different hangers as I explore the contents of Lucy's wardrobe. High-end designer labels and luxurious textures tease me. These clothes represent everything I envy about her life: the wealth, the status, and the unattainable perfection. "Everything you have should be mine," I hiss, my voice wavering with both anger and desire.

Most women would die to have what Lucy has. I shift my focus to her underwear drawer; Gilly Hicks, Victoria's Secret, Boux Avenue, Calvin Klein—all expensive and seductive. I wonder how many times Greg has seen her in these, his firm hands caressing her body as they lay entwined in each other's arms.

With a smile, I select a matching bra and knicker set, undressing and slipping into them. As I stretch out on Lucy's bed, I close my eyes and allow myself a few minutes of fantasy, imagining Greg's touch on my skin instead of my own during my lonely nights. The longing inside me builds, making my heart pound and my breath come in ragged gasps as I draw my fingers up the inside of my thighs.

"Greg," I say, before the reality of my situation snaps me back to the present as I rise from the bed. I take one last glance round the room before returning the borrowed lingerie and slipping on my own clothes. My pulse still races, but there's no time for distractions now. There's more work to be done as I check the time.

I retrace my steps, step out of the house, and leave the back door ajar.

Your life is about to get interesting, Lucy.

11

LUCY

I stare aimlessly, unsure what to think while I battle to clear my thoughts. I notice the tremor in my hands as I pour the wine, the bottle's neck clinking against the rim. Events from recent days have left me feeling shaken, and I'm desperate for something to take the edge off. Anything to help me calm my prickling skin and racing heart. I found the back door open again, but I'm sure it was locked. I dare not ask Greg again as he'll think I've really lost the plot.

"Lucy, do you really need that?" Greg's voice is steady, though his eyes are filled with concern. He stands by the door, watching me.

"It's just to calm down." I cradle the glass closer to my chest like a precious gift. "I've got it under control, Greg. Honestly."

My feels clammy beneath my blouse, and I feel the weight of his gaze on me. It's as if he's measuring my every move, scrutinising my decisions and deciding what he should do next.

"Lucy, I'm worried. This nanny thing and going back

to work has put too much pressure on you. You can't keep juggling everything and expect it to not go wrong."

"I won't quit work again," I say, shaking my head. "I can handle this. There have been some strange things happening lately, and I can't explain them." And it's true. Recent events have really freaked me out and the thought that someone may have been in my house terrifies me, and I'm scared to be on my own because of it. But I'm not going to tell Greg that.

"Strange things?" Greg frowns, taking a step closer. "What do you mean?"

I shake my head again, feeling the familiar knot of anxiety form in my stomach. "It's nothing. Just small things that don't add up. But I'm sure it's nothing to worry about."

"Lucy, you can't keep doing this. If something is bothering you, we need to deal with it together."

I take another small sip of my wine. "I know, but I can't exactly put my finger on it. I feel like I'm losing my mind, but I can't even explain why."

Greg studies me, his expression unreadable. "Okay, let's try to figure this out together. But promise me one thing: you won't brush off your worries like this again."

I nod, feeling a sense of relief wash over me. Maybe I'm not alone in this after all.

The room suddenly feels smaller as Greg moves closer to me and places his hands on my arms and studies me with a sceptical gaze. "Lucy, I want to believe you, but it sounds like you're allowing your imagination to go crazy."

"Greg, I'm not making this up." The words press out through gritted teeth. "These odd things are real; I know they are. Though I can't explain them, it doesn't mean they don't exist."

"Look, I understand that you're stressed, but we can't

jump at every little thing that seems off. We need to be rational and logical about this."

"Rational?" I huff, my hand tightening round the wine glass. "How can I be rational when I feel like I'm losing control of everything round me? And it's only me who sees it. You don't get it, do you? So why should I bother trying to make you understand?"

"Lucy, that's not fair," he protests, but I'm already turning my back on him. With a sigh, Greg retreats to the study, leaving me alone in the kitchen.

Hurt and angry, I pour myself another large glass of red, the dark liquid swirling like a vortex in the glass. Downing it in a few haphazard gulps, I try to push the feeling of loneliness, but it refuses to budge. The doorbell rings. Its chime jolts me from my thoughts, and I sway a little. I push aside my frustration as I open the door to Alice. Her soft brown eyes meet mine with a knowing look.

"Hi, Lucy. I hope I'm not too early," she says.

I swing the door wide. "Erm. Perfect timing. Come in."

Alice enters and drops her bag by the door as she greets the kids who have come running at the sound of her voice. They adore her, and it's easy to see why. She has a calming presence about her, something I envy more and more each day.

"Alright, little ones," she tells them, somehow capturing their full attention. "Let's go in the lounge and figure out what to do today, shall we?"

As Alice takes over, effortlessly guiding the children into the other room, I feel a twinge of guilt. Here I am, drowning in self-pity and alcohol while she steps in to save the day. I'm feeling like such a useless mum. "Thank you, Alice," I murmur when she passes by on her way to the lounge. She nods with a small, understanding smile.

"Of course. You know I'm always here to help," she replies.

Once they're settled, I retreat to the kitchen, where I pour myself another glass of wine. Leaning against the wall out of sight, I listen as Alice entertains the kids, her laughter mingling with theirs as they play some a made-up game. It's a bittersweet sound; a reminder of simpler times before this gnawing unease consumed me.

I take a furtive sip, the velvety liquid burning a fiery trail down my throat. It's not enough to drown out the nagging voice in my head, the one that insists I'm losing control. I can't keep going like this, drinking away my fears and pretending everything is fine when it so clearly isn't.

"Lucy?" Alice's voice startles me. I glance up to find her peering at me with concern. "Is everything okay?"

"Uh, yeah," I stammer, lowering my glass to my side. "I needed a moment to myself."

"Of course." Her gaze lingers on me for a moment longer before she returns to the kids. Despite her understanding, the weight of her unspoken judgement only makes me feel worse. The doorbell rings again. I hastily hide my wine glass behind a potted plant and make my way to the door.

As it swings open, I'm greeted by Beth's familiar face. "Hey, Lucy. I thought I'd drop by for a bit. Everything okay as I've not heard from you?"

"Sure, come in," I reply. The tense atmosphere in the house is palpable, and I can see Beth pick up on it as she steps inside and follows me through to the kitchen. Alice glances up from where she sits with the kids, offering a polite nod before returning to their game.

"Greg and I had a bit of a disagreement earlier," I confess, grabbing my wine glass from its hiding spot and draining the last of the wine. "He doesn't trust me, Beth.

He thinks I can't handle things and keeps pushing for me to give up work, even though I've just started back."

Beth frowns, her eyes flicking between the wine glass and my face. "I'm sorry, Luce. That must be really hard for you."

"Hard? It's bloody annoying," I shout, my voice rising in pitch as I gesture with the empty glass. "I've been trying so hard to keep everything together, and he... he doesn't believe in me."

"Calm down," Beth says softly, placing a hand on my arm. Her touch is gentle, but there's a firmness to it that shows her concern. "I know it's tough, but fighting with Greg isn't going to help anything."

I place my hand over my friend's. "Maybe not, but at least it's something. I can't sit here and pretend everything's fine when he's doubting me at every turn."

"I understand that you're upset," Beth begins, but I interrupt her.

"Upset? I'm furious. And hurt. You have no idea what it's like to feel so... so powerless in your own life." My voice cracks on the last word as the tears sting my eyes.

"I really think you should talk to Greg about this. He needs to understand how you're feeling," Beth suggests, her voice gentle but insistent.

"Maybe." I wipe away a stray tear. "But right now, I need the support of my friends."

"Of course." Beth wraps an arm round my shoulders and gives me a comforting squeeze. "We're here for you. Always. But Luce..." Beth's voice trails off. Her concern is clear as she furrows her brow. "Maybe you should slow down on the plonk. It won't help solve anything."

"Not you as well?" My grip on the wine glass tightens.

"I'm worried about you. This isn't like you. And it

probably won't help with Greg's trust issues if he sees you knocking back glass after glass."

"Greg doesn't trust me anyway. So what does it matter?" I say, my voice laced with bitterness.

"Because you're better than this." My friend's eyes plead with me. "You're strong, you're capable, you're a brilliant mum, a fantastic wife, and you can handle whatever life throws at you. You don't need to rely on booze to get you through it."

"Thanks for the vote of confidence," I retort, unable to keep the edge out of my voice. Her words feel like a patronising pat on the head, and I hate it. Especially since they're coming right on the heels of *his* words.

"Lucy, I'm your friend, and I love you, but I can't stand by and watch you do this to yourself. I'll be here when you're ready to talk, but right now, I need to head off."

"Sure," I mutter, looking away from her, my cheeks burning with shame and fury.

Beth hesitates for a moment, her eyes searching mine for any sign that I might change my mind. But with a heavy sigh, she nods and heads for the door.

As the sound of the door closing echoes through the house, I feel very alone again. The weight of everything that's happened pushes down on me like a ton of concrete and blindly, I reach for the wine bottle and stare at it.

12

ALICE -THE PAST

As I sit and watch Matthew and Sarah play, their chatter filling the room, I'm taken aback when Jordan and I were children. The memory rushes in, unbidden and insistent.

The sunlight filters through the trees as we play in our family's garden. My hair curled behind my ears, and his scruffy mop falling into his eyes.

"Come on, Jordan! Let's see who can climb the tree the fastest," I shout, my breath catching as I race ahead towards the back of the garden.

He glares at me, a scowl spreading across his face. "I don't want to race you," he growls, a hint of menace lacing his words. "Just leave me alone, Alice."

But I nag him further, hoping he'll give in. "Please, Jordan," I plead, my voice wavering. "I want to play with you."

"Fine. Maybe later." He kicks away his football in annoyance. "But don't follow me round like a lost puppy. I want to play by myself."

Despite the harshness in his tone, I try to remain positive. I watch him walk away, the distance between us growing with each step he takes. As I stand there fixed to the spot, I feel a pang of loneliness that cuts deep.

"Jordan," I call out once more. "Can't we—?"

"Shut up, Alice!" he shouts, whirling round to face me. Anger twisting his features. "Why can't you leave me alone? I don't want you around. Go away."

I let out a deep sigh and look down at the grass as the sting of rejection washes over me. But despite how he treats me, I will be so nice that Jordan must be nice back. One day, he'll play with me. And as I watch him disappear through the trees, I yearn to have my old brother back. The one I worship, not this mean shell of the carefree, adoring brother he once was.

I stand there for what feels like forever, alone in the garden with the sun casting dappled shadows on the ground. I try to keep myself busy, picking up random sticks and twirling them between my fingers, but I can't stop thinking about Jordan. *Maybe if I give him time alone.* I hope that a little space will be enough for him to change his mind about playing with me. I glance in the direction I last saw him, biting my lip. After a while, the sound of footsteps draws my attention as I see Jordan coming back. His face now softened. I smile as excitement bubbles within me.

"Hey, Alice," he says, his voice gentle and almost apologetic. "I'm sorry for shouting at you before. Do you want to play a game together?"

My heart leaps at his words, glad to have finally caught his attention. "Really?" I jump up and down as I clap my hands together, my eyes lighting up with excitement.

"Yeah." He smiles and extends a hand towards me. "Come on, let's go."

As our palms clasp together, we walk together, side by

side. The weight of loneliness lifts from my shoulders. Finally, I feel like I belong by my brother's side.

We settle down beneath a tree, and Jordan explains the rules of the game he wants us to play. I listen. Little do I know that this momentary happiness is fragile. But for now, I love the fun of interacting with my brother. And as we continue to play, I cling to the hope that my kindness will be enough to keep me connected to Jordan. The tree's leaves rustle above us as we start. I watch him carefully, and as the game progresses, he adds new random and cruel rules that suit only him so that he wins.

"Jordan," I say, "I don't think that rule was part of the game. It's not fair."

He glares at me, his eyes narrowing. "Yes, they were, Alice. You weren't listening." His voice is cold and hard.

"No, I just thought... maybe you forgot," I mumble, trying to get him to be fair.

"Look," he says, "if you will not play by my rules, then maybe I should find someone else to play with."

I give in, the fear and disappointment suffocating me. "Sorry, Jordan. I'll play by your rules."

"Good." On the heels of Jordan's knowing smirk, we return to the game. Why does he enjoy teasing me like this? What have I done to deserve it?

As the clock ticks, I feel the weight of defeat creeping up on me. Yet, despite it being unfair, I keep playing, hoping that my brother will come round and be nice.

But as each round passes, I keep losing, much to his amusement. Finally, the game ends, and I'm crushed as I bury my head in my hands to hide my tears. Jordan smirks, his eyes alight with cruel satisfaction. And in that moment, I realise that no matter how kind or understanding I try to be, it might never be enough to save him from himself.

"Fine," he says, a hint of mock kindness in his voice. "I'll let you keep playing... but you have to do what I want."

I smile and nod, desperate for any scrap of affection from my brother. He studies me for a moment, as though trying to gauge whether I'm sincere.

"Alright then." He leans back and folds his arms across his chest. "Pick up that piece there and move it forward three spaces."

My hand trembles as I reach for the game piece, the coldness of its surface against my fingertips. Is this another cruel trick? Another way for him to hurt me?

"Good." When I've completed the move, I see something different in his eyes. A fleeting warmth that disappears as he moves his piece. "Your turn," he adds with a smirk.

As we continue the game, I find myself torn between hope and despair as Jordan swings between moments of kindness and hurtful remarks.

"Move your piece there," he commands, pointing to a spot on the board with a sneer. "Or are you too stupid to understand?"

"Please, don't be mean," I say through gritted teeth, struggling to hold back tears. "I'm only trying to play the game with you, Jordan."

"Shut up and move your piece." At his harsh command, I obey, getting upset as the tears blur my vision.

"Got you. You're out," Jordan declares with a wicked smile, and I feel the last of my hopes crumble away.

"Fine, you win." Choking back sobs, I struggle to get the words out.

"I always do." His laugh is cold and cruel.

"Ah, Alice, it's so nice to see you two playing together,"

Mum says from the doorway, her voice like an unexpected ray of sunlight.

"Hey, Mum," Jordan replies with a charming smile that doesn't quite reach his eyes. "We're enjoying a friendly game of stones."

"Good." Her gaze lingers on me. She searches my face for signs of distress, but I push out a weak smile, not wanting her to see the pain. With a satisfied look, she turns away, leaving us alone once more.

"Remember, if you don't let me win, I'll never let you play with me again," Jordan says through his grin.

"Alright, I promise," I agree.

"Good doggie," he mocks.

"Jordan," I begin, my voice soft and tentative, "thank you."

His eyes narrow, and he studies me with suspicion. "What are you going on about?"

"Nothing. Thank you for spending time with me, even though I know... I know you don't want to."

Jordan tosses his head back and laughs. "You're right. I don't want to."

But then, a flicker of defiance sparks within me, refusing to be extinguished. I won't give up on my brother, no matter how horrible he is to me right now. This is just a stage he's going through. It has to be. As long as he's my brother, I will keep looking for a way to bridge the gap between us.

"Jordan," I look him straight in the eye, "one day, you'll see that I only want us to be happy."

He laughs and shakes his head. "Alice, you stupid idiot. Don't you understand? I'm the older brother. You do what I say."

I get up and run back into the house and to my bedroom, his cruel laughter fading into the distance.

13

LUCY

The scent of Alice's freshly brewed coffee fills the air as I gather up stray toys and bits of paper scattered across the kitchen. My nanny, with her hair tied back in a neat ponytail, hums while loading the dishwasher for me. I could get used to this.

"Thanks for helping me with this mess, Alice." My words come out like rapid fire as they often do when I'm stressed and tired. "The kids have been such a handful."

"It's no problem, honestly, Lucy," she replies in her soft, considerate tone. "I know you have a lot on your plate." Alice laughs as she stares at the plate in her hand.

As we chat, Alice listens and doesn't judge, providing the perfect listening companion. Still, the headaches, foggy head, and tiredness that have been plaguing me for the past few days now refuse to go, leaving me irritable and anxious.

"Could you entertain the kids for a moment?" A hint of desperation creeps into my voice. "I need a quick break."

"Sure." She wipes her hands and heads towards the lounge. "We can work on spellings or something."

With Alice distracting the little ones, I sneak into the larder. There, I reach for the open bottle of red wine I've been nursing for the past week. It's become my crutch, my way of coping with the overwhelming stress and anxiety that grips me. As I take a gulp, the rich liquid warming my throat, I shut my eyes and push away the feelings that surface. The mixture of shame, guilt, and fear tangles with my ever-present headaches, forming a dark cloud over my thoughts. As much as I want to stop drinking, I can't bring myself to face the reality of my life without a form of escape.

"Lucy?" Alice's voice, soft yet concerned, pulls me back to now as I take one more glug and replace the bottle alongside the others. "Are you alright?"

"Fine," I lie, forcing a smile onto my face as I reappear. "Just needed a moment to check what I need to add to my shopping list."

"Alright." Alice's eyes are still filled with worry. "You don't look too well. Maybe you're coming down with a bug?"

"Maybe." I rub my forehead and feel the dizziness increasing with each passing moment. "I think I need to lie down for a bit."

"Of course. I'll watch the kids. You get some rest and shout down if you need anything."

"Thank you," I murmur as I make my way up the stairs, clinging to the bannister as the world seems to tip and sway round me. From the bottom of the stairs, Alice watches me with concern before she disappears into the lounge to join the children.

When I reach my bedroom, I collapse onto the bed, the cool sheets soothing my hot skin. Sleep claims me within minutes, dragging me under its blanket of darkness. One so heavy no matter how hard I try to lift my lids, they stay shut.

I can't remember anything after that, but upon waking, I check the bedside and gasp in shock to find that I've been asleep for nearly two hours. Confused, I sit up, rubbing my eyes before noticing the small bottle of red wine on the bedside table. I can't remember bringing it up here, and the sight of it horrifies me as I look round to make sure that no one is in the bedroom with me. Scared of its presence, like a poisoned chalice, I jump out of bed. I grab it and jam it in the wardrobe among the heaps of shoes in the bottom; I can't risk anyone seeing it.

My head feels like I have stuffed it with cotton wool, and my legs feel like lead weights as I stagger round the bedroom. My chest feels tight. A sharp, metallic taste lingers in my mouth as I lick my lips, adding to the disorientation. Why did I drink so much? And why can't I remember?

With a deep sigh, I run my hand through my hair and straighten my clothes to clean up my appearance. I know I need to rejoin Alice and the children downstairs, but the dizziness and confusion continue to haunt me, making every step feel like a battle against my body and mind. My heart thuds in my chest, heavy and erratic. I stare at my reflection in the mirror and wonder what's happening to me. This isn't right. My cheeks are flushed, and my eyes are glassy, bloodshot, and unfocused. With trembling hands, I splash cold water on my face in an attempt to make sense of the haze clouding my mind.

"Lucy?" Alice's voice drifts up from downstairs, pulling me back to reality. "Dinner's ready."

"Coming," I call out, forcing a smile into my voice. But inside, I'm reeling.

As I descend the stairs, I grip the bannister. My legs are like jelly beneath me. My stomach churns like a cement mixer, ready to unload its contents. I pause on the bottom step and take a final big breath before stepping into the dining room.

"Everything alright?" Alice asks when I join her, Greg, and the kids, her gaze flicking over me with concern.

"Fine," I lie, my voice croaky. "Tired. I was zonked out."

The enticing aroma of spag bol fills the air as we sit down to eat, but my appetite has vanished. I pick at my food, struggling to focus on the conversation round me. My thoughts keep circling back to the bottle of wine hidden upstairs and the unsettling sensation that I'm simply not right.

"Luce, you're not eating much. Are you okay, sweetheart?" Greg remarks, his brow furrowed with worry.

"I'm not very hungry," I mumble, pushing the side salad round my plate. "Must be coming down with something."

"Maybe you should rest after dinner." He stretches out his hand to touch mine, but the warmth of his touch only serves to heighten my guilt.

As the meal wears on, I grow more and more disoriented. My speech slurs, my movements become clumsy as the fork slips from my hand several times, and my vision blurs in and out of focus. It's as if I'm far drunker than I should be, given the small amount I recall drinking.

"Lucy, are you alright?" my husband asks. I open my mouth to speak, but my words come out slurred, barely comprehensible.

"Just... tired," I mumble, feeling humiliated. Alice watches me from her seat, her cheeks flushed with embarrassment for me. This isn't what she signed up for when she agreed to help us.

"Maybe you should go back to bed." Greg's disappointment is palpable, and it cuts through me like a knife. I don't want him to think I'm spiralling into old habits.

I nod, trying to push away the fear and confusion crowding my mind. "Yeah, I... I think you're right," I murmur as I rise to my feet.

"Seriously, Lucy," Alice insists, her eyes wide with worry. "You don't look very well at all. Go rest. We'll take care of everything down here."

"Alright," I concede, defeated. With a heavy heart, I push away from the table and stagger. Greg reaches across to grab my arm.

"Let me help you upstairs," Alice offers, already moving towards me. But I ignore her offer, determined to maintain my dignity.

"No, I can manage." With my voice wavering, Alice is insistent. I glance at Greg, who remains silent, as I stumble away and begin the agonising journey up the stairs. Each step feels like climbing a mountain, my head threatening to split apart from the pressure inside. The metallic taste in my mouth tastes worse, sending waves of nausea through me. What's happening to me? Is this the result of too much wine? Or is it a bug?

Everything spins round me, and I cling to the walls for support as I make it back to my bedroom. As I collapse onto my bed, the questions continue to swarm in my mind as I stare at the ceiling. How did I get here?

14

ALICE

I close the bedroom door and make my way downstairs where I find Greg by the last step with his hands buried in the pockets of his trousers and a deep furrow etched between his brows. As I approach him, he looks tired and weary.

"Greg, is everything alright?"

He shakes his head before sighing. "I'm worried about Lucy. She's not been herself lately, and I'm worried she's slipping back into old habits."

"Old habits?"

Greg rubs his face. "Lucy doesn't cope well with stress. In the past, when things got too much for her, she'd... drown her sorrows." He takes a steadying breath before continuing. "We lost our first baby, you see. It hit her hard; she fell into a terrible depression lasting for months. She hid a lot of it. The meds helped her to cope, and they were a lifesaver, but she lost so much of her personality. Hardly left the house. Didn't speak to anyone. Cried in bed, hugging her pillow. That's when she started drinking in secret."

"I had no idea," I say. "But I promise I'll keep an eye on her when you're not around. I'll do whatever I can to help you both. Remember I'm here to support you too. You're not doing this alone. I'm always at the end of the phone."

"Thank you, Alice." He smiles and nods before walking me to the door.

"Goodnight, Greg." I squeeze his arm as I pass him.

As I walk away into the darkness, a small smile plays on my lips.

15

LUCY

I force my eyelids open and blink hard. The morning light blinds my vision for a few moments. My head pounds while I work to shake off the heavy feeling of sleep.

Dragging from my bed, I stumble into the bathroom and stand under the lukewarm spray of the shower. The water does little to clear my mind, but at least it washes away the sweat that clings to my body. I wipe away the condensation from the mirror and stare at the reflection of a pale, pathetic thing with haunted eyes and hollow cheeks who's unrecognisable as the woman I was a few weeks ago.

Dressed for work, I head to the kitchen. The confusion from last night lingers as I open the larder door once more. What I see makes no sense. Four small bottles of red wine sitting on the shelf. But there were only four when I took one yesterday evening. Did I not take one? Did I replace it? I don't remember while I grapple with deciding what is real and what is a figment of my broken mind?

"Morning, Lucy," Alice calls out as she opens the front door and breezes into the kitchen. She takes off her jacket and places it on the back of one of the dining table chairs. Her eyes narrow and her lips tighten into a thin line. "You still don't look too good. Are you feeling alright? You seemed quite tired and unwell last night."

"Morning, Alice." I force a weak smile. "I must have caught a bug. But I'm feeling better now. Thanks for asking." I close the larder door, trying to hide the uneasiness and twisting knots in my stomach. Did I imagine the whole thing?

"Are you sure? You don't seem yourself."

"Really, I'm fine," I insist. "Just stressed with work and everything, you know?" My voice wobbles. I want to confide in her, to share what's been happening, but a small voice in the back of my mind says that she might not understand, and it's not a good idea for my nanny to think I'm really mad.

"Alright, as long as you're sure," she says, though her eyes still hold worry. "Just remember, if you need someone to talk to, I'm here for you."

"Thank you." I manage a more genuine smile this time. "I appreciate it."

"Why don't you take a day off and stay home with the kids? You might need the rest."

"I'd love to." I glance at the clock on the wall. "But I have an important face-to-face meeting at work today. I can't afford to miss it." I grab my purse and mobile phone from the counter and slide it into my pocket. "Really, I'll be fine," I insist, though my pounding headache and the lingering fog in my mind tell me I'm not right.

"Alright. Just promise me you'll take care of yourself."

"Promise," I reply, before giving her a quick hug.

"Thank you for being here for me. And for looking after the kids. It means the world to me."

"It's my pleasure. You know I'm always here for you and your family," she says softly, returning the embrace.

With that, I head out the door, forcing myself to focus on the day ahead. While part of me wishes I could stay behind and sort through the mess in my head, I know I can't avoid the responsibilities of my job any longer.

16

ALICE

THE WOODS BEHIND THE BUTLERS' house have been a sanctuary for me and a perfect place to watch them. I rarely see anyone, so I can stand in the shadows for hours watching the family in the garden or see family life being played out through their patio doors. But today, they provide a chance for me to take Matthew and Sarah out for a short walk round the woods, listening for the birds in the trees and spotting squirrels racing along branches or scurrying round on the ground looking for food.

"Alice," a voice calls out, snapping me back to reality. I look up to see Beth approaching, her dog wagging its tail excitedly by her side.

"Hey, Beth. How are you?"

"Good, thanks. But I'm more worried about Lucy. How is she?"

"Ah, yeah. She's been under the weather, that's all. Nothing to worry about."

"Are you sure?" Beth's troubled gaze locks with mine. "You know you can talk to me if something's bothering you, right?"

I hesitate for a moment, unsure whether to confide in her. But I need to play the game and look concerned. "Actually, Beth... She's been having these strange episodes," I begin, my voice shaking slightly for effect. "She keeps losing chunks of time, and her memories are all jumbled. It's like she's not all there and together, if that makes sense?"

Beth listens, her brow furrowing in sympathy. "That sounds awful. Do you think it could be related to stress, or maybe even alcohol? I know you mentioned finding empty wine bottles."

"Maybe."

"Alice," Beth says softly, "I care about Lucy and her family, and I want to help. But she needs to be honest with herself and the people round her. If there's something going on, whether it's stress, alcohol, or even something else, we can't support her if we don't know what's happening."

"Thank you, Beth. I'm glad Lucy has such a good friend looking out for her."

The dampness of the woods surrounds us, leaves sticking to my boots as Beth and I walk further along the narrow path, the kids trotting a few steps ahead of us.

"Greg's struggling," I say, my voice lowering. God, I'm so good at the acting thing. I should be on TV. "He tries to be strong for the kids, but I can see how much it's affecting him. Lucy won't listen to him."

Beth nods, her eyes fixed on the ground as we tread through a muddy patch. "I've noticed that too. It's such a shame."

"None of them do. But what can we do? Lucy's not open to talking about her problems." A breeze whips through the trees, sending shivers down my spine. I wrap my arms round myself, trying to hold onto the warmth of my coat.

"I'll talk to her."

"Thanks. I know it's difficult to confront a friend, especially one as stubborn as Lucy. But I believe she needs our help, whether or not she wants to admit it."

As we exit the woods and make our way back towards the Butlers' house, I sense a renewed purpose in Beth as she splits off from me and heads to her front door. And even though I played my part to perfection, that concerns me. I don't need Beth getting in the way of my plans.

17

LUCY

As I drive home, my mind is a million miles away from the steady hum of the engine. My boss's words ring in my ears: "You've been so distracted, Lucy. It's not like you." I slap my hand on the steering wheel as my frustration rises. Even she's doubting me now? The sound of my own angry voice fills my head, drowning out all else.

Lost in thought, I barely register the sudden swerve of my car across the road into oncoming traffic. Panic courses through me as I jerk the wheel to correct my direction, narrowly avoiding the high beams and horn from an approaching car. Shit. Panicked, I pull over and come to a stop, my hands shaking on the wheel, my eyes wide in shock. I let out a shaky breath, trying to compose myself.

"Jesus! What am I doing? What is wrong with me?" I say under my breath as I glance round and then restart the car and carry on my journey home.

Once on the drive, I switch off the engine and grab my bag. As I enter the house I slam the door behind me and head straight upstairs to change, barely registering Greg and Alice in the lounge. I pull my earrings out, reaching for my jewellery box to place them inside, but it's not there. I frown as I look round. It's not on the dresser top or in the drawers. Where is it? I know I left it here this morning.

I tear round my room, tossing pillows and clothes aside, but I can't find it. It makes little sense—I saw it this morning. *It has to be here somewhere.* I sit on the bed in resignation, my chest heaving with frustration. The missing box feels like just another piece of the puzzle in my screwed-up life. But I can't dwell on it; I need to find it.

I push off the bed, continuing my search.

"Greg. Alice!" I yell, storming down the stairs. "Have either of you seen my jewellery box?"

"Your what?" Greg asks.

"My jewellery box. It's not in our bedroom, and I know I left it there this morning. Have you moved it?" I say, my voice tight as I jab a finger towards the stairs.

"I've not seen it, but we can look together," Alice offers. She follows me back upstairs, her steps soft and in stark contrast to my own heavy stomps.

"See? It's not here." I plant my hands on my hips as I look at the mess I've made.

"Let's check again. It must be here somewhere." Alice searches the wardrobes.

"Fine," I mutter, as I join her in looking round the room once again. I can't seem to shake the unsettling feeling that something strange is happening...

"I found it," Alice calls out after a few minutes, pulling the jewellery box out from under the bed where it was hidden beneath a crumpled shirt. "It must have been on the floor and been pushed under as you or Greg were passing."

"Or someone moved it," I say, unable to keep my suspicions hidden. But Alice smiles kindly at me, her expression empathetic as Greg stands in the doorway.

"It's a simple mistake to make, Lucy. You're tired from yesterday." She hands me the box with a slight touch on my arm. As she leaves the room, she throws Greg a look of concern, which I catch out of the corner of my eye. Are they are both judging me?

"Thank you, Alice." My voice is strained as I clutch the jewellery box tightly in my hands. "I... I'm not losing it, I promise."

"Of course not, Lucy." With a reassuring smile, Alice disappears downstairs. And yet, as I stand there in the wreckage of my bedroom, Am I losing my mind?

The door clicks shut behind Alice, leaving Greg and me alone in the bedroom. I can feel his eyes on me, scrutinising every move I make as I place my earrings and necklace into the jewellery box. The air between us is thick with unspoken tension.

"Lucy," he begins cautiously, rubbing his brow as if trying to smooth out the creases of concern etched there. "I'm worried about you. Look at the state of this room now. It's like a bomb has gone off in here."

"Is that so?" It's hard not to feel defensive when everyone seems to conspire against me. "And what exactly are you worried about, Greg?"

"Your... behaviour lately." He hesitates as if searching for the right words. "The forgetfulness, the tiredness, the paranoia... I think maybe we should talk to someone, get some help."

"Help?" I scoff, my hands clenching into fists by my sides. "You think I need help? Just because I misplaced a bloody jewellery box?"

"Lucy, it's not just that," he insists. "It's everything.

You're taking on too much, you react to the slightest thing, and you're drinking again. You even left the tap running in the sink this morning. It's not like you."

"Maybe it's because I'm being got at, Greg. I didn't leave the tap running." As I march towards him and stand inches away my anger boils over. "Have you ever considered someone might be messing with me, making me doubt myself?"

"Listen to yourself." His tone borders on exasperation. I don't like it. Not one bit. Sometimes he's so insufferable I wonder why I married him. "We're supposed to be a team, you and me. But how can we work together if you don't trust me or Alice?"

"Trust has to be earned, Greg," I snap. "And right now, I don't know who or what to trust anymore."

Greg steps back, his eyes wide with shock. "Luce, please," he pleads. "I love you, and I want what's best for you, but I can't help you if you won't let me in."

Frustration and hurt cause my whole body to tremble. "I don't need your help! I need someone to believe me when I say that something isn't right!"

"Alright. If that's what you want, then I'll try my best to understand," Greg murmurs softly, taking a step back again as if retreating from the battlefield that our marriage has become.

"Good." I inhale a breath, wiping angrily at the tears that threaten to spill over. "Because I'm not going crazy. I know what's happening to me is real, even if no one else does."

"Fine. If you're so sure that something's going on, then you should take the time off work. Clear your head, figure things out. Get a blood test. Perhaps you're running low on something like iron and that's making you fatigued and giving you a fuzzy head?"

I feel my chest tighten at his suggestion, and the insinuation that I'm overworked and imagining things like a hysterical woman. But just as quickly, the defensiveness fades, replaced by a bone-deep weariness. "Yes. Perhaps you're right. I'll see if I can get a doctor's appointment." I know it takes a few days of trying to get an appointment as they all disappear within minutes of the surgery lines opening at eight a.m., but I have to try.

With a heavy sigh, Greg comes to me and kisses my forehead and tells me that he loves me, before turning, pausing only to grab his gym kit from its usual spot on the hook beside the wardrobe. "I need to clear my head too," he mutters, his voice strained with emotion. "Going to the gym might help. Is that okay, or would you like me to stay?"

"No, it's okay. Thank you for offering. Love you too." I watch him leave the room with a sense of isolation. It feels like I'm glued in place as I watch us drift apart. The door clicks shut behind him, leaving me with my thoughts, my doubts, and the ever-present fear that my world is slipping through my fingers like sand.

I sit down heavily on the edge of our bed, the mattress sagging beneath my weight. Nothing makes sense. Is all this a product of stress, exhaustion, or something worse? But deep down I know there's something deeper than that. The missing jewellery box, the odd behaviour from Alice and Greg—it's all connected somehow. And as I sit there in the gloom of our once-happy home, one thing is clear: no one's coming to save me.

I have to figure it out alone.

But first, I will take Greg's advice and step away from work. A little distance might help me see things more clearly. My company has been great so far, welcoming me back into my old role and giving me the time to adjust. It's not ideal to take time off so soon after starting back, but I hope they'll understand.

18

LUCY

WITH ALICE GONE and Greg at the gym, I'm home alone again. I stand by my bedroom window, emptying the laundry basket to keep my mind occupied. The silence of the house feels claustrophobic even though the kids are in their bedrooms. Picking up Greg's jeans, I check the pockets. I hate it when a rogue tissue gets caught up in the washing and leaves a white scattering of tissue flecks on everything else. As I do this, my gaze drifts out of the window towards the dark blanket of the woods behind our house.

My fingers catch on something unexpected, a small pouch in one of the back pockets. But before I can check it further, my heart lurches as I notice movement in the treeline out back. I freeze, dropping Greg's jeans back into the basket with a soft thud.

"Is that...?" I blink hard, trying to clear my vision, my mouth hanging open in shock. A moving shadow in the trees beside our fence. My pulse quickens with every beat. "No, it can't be," I say to myself, my voice tinged with fear. But the more I stare, the more certain I am that someone's out there. Someone watching us. I know there have been a few burglaries in the area in recent months, and with so many houses backing onto the woods, it's proved a useful escape route according to the neighbourhood police team.

Don't be daft. You're just seeing things.

I look away, focusing instead on the discarded jeans and the mysterious pouch. But the image of that shadowy figure won't leave my mind and the feeling of being watched. I look again, but there's nothing there... is there? Just dark shapes. Tree trunks surely? Maybe it's branches swaying and playing tricks on my mind. I try to be sensible, but the figure seemed too solid, too human-like to be a trick of the shadows.

With one last glance at the window, I race downstairs, pull the phone from my pocket and fling open the back door, the cool night air hitting my flushed face as I step outside. The darkness suffocates me, the shadows of the trees beyond our garden encroaching my personal space. Heart hammering in my chest, adrenaline propels me to the end of the garden where I peer over our low fence into the woods. After investigating the area with my phone's torchlight, I find nothing—no movement or evidence of anyone lurking about. The more I search, the more I doubt myself. Maybe it was the branches swaying in the darkness or deer. I've seen a few in the past.

"Hello?" I shout. Nothing. "Anyone there?" Still nothing but the faint rustling of leaves.

I rush back inside, feeling a shiver down my back. Locking the door behind me, I return to my bedroom, the lingering unease still sitting with me. As I move closer to the window, my eyes scan the darkened treeline, and once more, I'm sure I spot a shadowy figure standing at the edge of the woods. My body tenses. Panic sets in, overwhelming my senses as I fumble for my phone.

"Greg," I gasp when he answers, "please come home. The figure... it's back. There's someone outside in the woods."

There's a long pause. "I'm not long out of the shower, but I'll be there soon," Greg finally replies, his calm tone a stark contrast to my frantic one. "Keep the doors locked and call the police if anyone comes near the house. It might just be a homeless person trudging through. Do you remember there was something about a few homeless guys sleeping rough in the woods on our street's WhatsApp group?"

"Yes, maybe. Okay, but please hurry anyway," I plead, trying to keep an eye on the figure as I speak. But in the blink of an eye, it vanishes once more. As I wait for Greg, my thoughts race, then gallop out of control. I check on the kids and then fly down the stairs to double-check the front and rear doors. My overwrought mind wills him to hurry as I pace round the lounge. It feels like hours have passed once I hear Greg's car pulling up. My impatience grows with every passing second, waiting for him to come inside. It seems like an eternity until I hear laughter drifting in from outside.

"Really? Now?" I say. I march towards the front door and yank it open. My mouth falls open at the sight of Greg standing by his car talking to Beth, both smiling as they chat. They don't seem to notice me at first, but when they do, Greg's expression shifts to concern.

"Lucy, I'm so sorry." He excuses himself from Beth and comes over to me. "Are you alright?"

"Am I alright?" My voice trembles with fear and frustration. "No, Greg, I'm not bloody alright. There's someone out there."

"Okay, let's take a look." Greg heads to the kitchen, grabbing a torch along the way. We step outside together.

As Greg searches the perimeter of our house and the treeline at the bottom of our garden, I stand near the doorway, my arms wrapped round myself, trying to shield myself from the chill. My gaze darts to the shadows cast by the trees.

"Lucy, I can't find any signs of anyone being here," Greg calls out.

"There's someone out there."

My husband's voice softens as he moves closer and wraps an arm around my shoulder. "It could have been shadows and trees."

"Shadows and trees don't move like that." I grip his arm. "Can we stay up and watch from the bedroom window for a bit? I need to know I'm not imagining it."

Greg hesitates, his eyes searching mine for a moment before he sighs and nods. "Alright. I'll keep watch with you, but if we don't see anything, you need to get some rest, okay? It was probably one of the homeless fellas. It would probably be a good idea if we get a Ring floodlight cam fitted to the back of the house. I've been meaning to look into those for a while now. They're triggered by motion, and we get alerts on our phones immediately. That will give us both peace of mind, don't you think?"

"Okay, good idea."

"I'll order it tomorrow." Greg places a hand around my waist as we head inside.

We stand together in our bedroom, our eyes glued to the shadowy woods. Greg's calm and steady presence is a comfort for me as he squeezes my hands every so often. Hours pass, and the world outside remains still. The shadows cast by trees sway in the breeze. I watch every movement in anticipation of the mysterious figure's return. A screeching fox breaks the silence and makes me jump. But as the clock ticks on, tiredness takes over and I can sense my body sag.

"Lucy," Greg murmurs, nudging me gently. "You're falling asleep. I think it's time to call it a night."

"Please, just a bit longer." Rubbing my eyes, I push myself to stay awake.

"We've been at this for hours. There's nothing there," Greg murmurs, his voice strained from staying awake.

"But... what if it comes back?" I ask.

"Then we'll deal with it," he replies, coaxing me to our bed. "But right now, you need sleep. We both do. Come on. We've been looking for ages and we haven't seen anything unusual."

"Can you leave the bedside lamp on?" I say, unable to cope with the darkness.

"Yep," Greg sighs, before climbing into bed beside me. I curl into this body and throw my arm over him, welcoming the safety it gives me. I close my eyes and try to push the images from my mind until exhaustion finally takes hold, pulling me under into a restless sleep.

19

ALICE

The scent of decaying leaves fills the air, and the damp earth beneath my feet clings to my shoes as I hide in the shadows of the woods near the Butlers' house. Only an hour ago, that nosey old fart Stanley Roberts caught me as he traipsed through the woods on his security patrol. He'd spotted me close to the Butlers' rear garden, his beady eyes narrowing with suspicion.

"Oi, what are you doing here?" he'd demanded, his voice gruff and accusatory.

"Mr Roberts," I'd stammered, trying to keep my composure. "I'm Alice, the nanny for the Butlers. Just out for a stroll after a long day looking after their children."

He'd eyed me warily, but I saw the doubt in his eyes wane. "Alright. Just be careful. These woods aren't safe at night. Anyone could lurk about and there are plenty of weirdos out there."

"I'll be very careful. I just needed a bit of fresh air," I'd replied. Then I forced a smile thinking that if he only knew I was one of those weirdos.

As we went our separate ways, he kept glancing over

his shoulder at me, making me question if he believed me. To avoid bumping into him again, I waited an hour before returning to my spot in the woods.

Now, as I stand here, the cold and isolation that surrounds me feels like a familiar friend. One that has been by my side for most of my life. It neither scares nor comforts me.

It just is.

I spot Lucy looking out as she sifts through the dirty washing. *Will she find the condom tonight?* I laugh to myself. It excites me to see the terror on her face as she comes racing out into the garden looking for any signs of a stalker. I feel like screaming like a wild banshee to really scare the pants off her, but I don't want to push her so far that she calls the police. I'm too quick for her as I step back further into the trees, listening to her call out. And then we do it all again once Greg arrives. Through the branches and shadows, I watch as the beam from a torch dances round in the darkness. I crouch behind dense bushes and pull my coat hood over my head to blend into the darkness.

A light goes on in an upstairs bedroom, and I see Lucy and Greg standing by the window, silence between them as they stare stony-faced into the darkness.

As I study them, my thoughts wander to when it all started. The birth of my plan, my thirst for revenge. As a young adult, I spent countless hours in the library poring over child psychology books, trying to understand the minds of children and their needs. It was there that I realised I could use this information to infiltrate the lives of families like the Butlers, armed with the information I needed to gain their trust. My mind drifts back to that fateful day.

The librarian peered at me over her computer when I

asked her where to find the books on child development and parenting. Then she guided me through the aisles to the right section. As I sat there absorbing every word, a seed was planted in my mind, a seed that would grow into a sinister plot.

With revenge on my mind, I began applying to nanny job listings. Each application was crafted to highlight my knowledge and understanding of children's emotional, physical, and psychological needs, as well as my ability to adapt to different family dynamics.

My efforts paid off as interviews turned into job offers, and I worked in the homes of unsuspecting families. With each new position, I grew better at manipulating the trust placed in me. I cared for their children with unwavering dedication, my every action driven by a dark purpose they could never understand. And as my reputation grew, so too did the web of deceit I spun round me. But it was never enough. The image of Jordan haunted my every waking moment.

The chance to attend a conference for childcare professionals later in my career gave me the opportunity to position myself as an elite nanny. Of course I jumped at the opportunity and the memory still sends shivers down my spine.

I entered the conference hall, a hive of activity as nannies and childcare professionals mingled and exchanged advice. As I wormed my way through the crowd, I tuned in on conversations and listened, searching for any opportunity that might bring me closer to the Butlers.

"Excuse me," I said, approaching a well-dressed woman. "I couldn't help overhearing your conversation about the exclusive nanny agency. I'm Alice, by the way."

"Ah, yes. I'm Meg." She extended her hand. "It's always nice to meet another dedicated professional."

"Likewise." Our hands met, and I forced a smile. "I've been working with several wonderful families, but I'm always looking for new opportunities to grow and learn. I'd love to hear more if you don't mind," I said, handing her my CV.

"Of course." Meg glanced over my details and outlined a few roles, discussing the stringent requirements and the high-end families it catered to.

"Sounds fascinating," I said.

As Meg continued talking, I glanced round the room, observing the other attendees.

"Remember, first impressions are crucial," Meg pointed out, bringing my attention back to our conversation. "Parents are looking for someone who exudes confidence and professionalism. You need to show them you're the perfect fit for their family from the very beginning."

"Absolutely," I agreed, nodding. "Thank you for your insight, Meg." My hand dipped into my bag, retrieving a pen and a small notebook. I scribbled down her words, adding them to the extensive list of phrases I'd accumulated over the years.

"Anytime, Alice," she replied, smiling.

As our conversation ended, I thanked Meg, knowing more about what I needed to do to become the ideal nanny.

Not long after, I started watching the Butlers from a distance, my car parked far enough away to not raise suspicion. I went to their house often and it was rare that I'd see either of them. But one night I did. The dim light from the street lamps threw elongated shadows on the pavement as I wrapped my coat round me and sipped coffee from a flask, ready for another night. The hours were long, but I kept myself busy talking to Jordan. He didn't always reply when I asked him a question, but I knew he was listening even if he pretended to ignore me. And as day broke, the familiar figure of Greg Butler appeared from his front door.

"Off to work again, Mr Butler?" I said to myself, watching as he climbed into his car, briefcase in hand. I felt a growing sense of resentment towards him. He represented the very thing I hated: privilege, wealth, and complacency.

And so, here I am now in my usual spot, standing in the shadows of the night. Just like all the times before. My thoughts drift to Lucy as I replay the conversations I've had with her in my head. Her pathetic and false gestures and sickening voice paint ghoulish pictures in my mind, making me feel like I'm right there with her, ready to punch her pretty face. My heart aches for the family she's trying so hard to keep together.

I vow to myself that I won't fail Jordan again. "You didn't deserve this. Jordan, I promise you, I'll make this right," I say to myself, clenching my fists as I stare at their house once more before disappearing into the night.

20

LUCY

THE FRONT DOOR slams shut behind me, the sound echoing through our home as I return from work. I drop my bag on the floor and clench my hands into fists as I try to calm myself.

"Lucy. What's wrong?" Greg calls from the lounge. He appears in the doorway, his eyes searching mine for answers as he leans in and kisses my cheek.

"You won't believe what happened today. Someone scratched the entire side of my car while I was in the office." My voice rises to almost a screech.

"Scratched? How bad is it?"

"Bad enough that it's clearly deliberate. I don't know what I've done, or who I've upset, but someone is targeting me, Greg. And I'm certain of one thing: they won't stop until they've pushed me over the bloody edge." The words tumble out, my mind racing in my attempt to make sense of it all.

"Surely it could have just been an accident." He reaches for my hand, attempting to offer comfort, but I snatch it away.

"An accident? It looks like someone took a bloody big key to it—this isn't just a random scratch. This was done on purpose." I can feel my eyes welling up.

"Come here, Luce." Greg pulls me into his arms, and I let him this time, my body softening in his embrace. "We'll figure this out. You're safe and that's all that matters. These things can be repaired easily. I can get someone like ChipsAway to come here to repair it. A few hours and it will look like new."

Greg always comes up with solutions, and I appreciate it as I nod into his chest.

He strokes my hair. "Did you park too close to a neighbouring car and didn't notice? And as that car pulled out, it scratched yours. It's easy to happen."

I step back and look at Greg, my brows pinches in the middle. I have to run it through my mind once more to be sure I heard him right. "Are you seriously implying that I'd be so careless that I parked it so recklessly that it would get damaged?" I roll my eyes in disbelief. "I'm not that absent-minded, Greg. And I would remember if I'd done something like that."

"I'm just trying to consider all the possibilities. Parking spaces seem to be tighter these days." He sighs, looking into my eyes with what seems like genuine concern. "I don't want you to jump to conclusions about someone targeting you when there might be another reasonable explanation."

"Jumping to conclusions?" Is he for real? "This isn't just a random event. Everything has been going wrong lately and I refuse to believe it's all just a coincidence. Maybe Alice has got it in for me."

Greg shakes his head and throws me a half-hearted smile. "Alright," he concedes, raising his hands in surrender. "I doubt she has anything to do with it. Let's go outside and take a closer look at the car together, okay?"

As we step out onto the drive, the damage to the car is glaringly obvious.

"See?" I gesture towards the scratches. "I didn't do this. I'm a good driver. I wouldn't have caused this much damage and not known about it."

"I didn't say you did it on purpose," he replies, his voice strained and laced with frustration. "But perhaps it was an accident."

"An accident?" I scoff, shaking my head in disbelief. "Someone is targeting me. Can't you see that?"

He reaches out, but I move away. "Okay, it doesn't look great. We'll get it fixed." He walks round the car, bending occasionally to inspect the damage close up as he runs his finger along the score marks and shrugs before ushering me back in. "I want to show you something."

I follow Greg into the kitchen, my curiosity piqued, and I'm not sure why he's bringing me back into the kitchen without uttering another word.

"Look at this." My husband points towards the sink, where a few empty red wine bottles stand. "I found these round the house, Lucy. You've been secretly drinking again."

My blood runs cold, and my mouth runs dry. I clench my jaw tightly, trying to steady myself. "You don't trust me. I don't have a drinking problem any more. And I didn't scratch the car. And I certainly didn't drink all that wine."

He sighs heavily, pinching the bridge of his nose in frustration. "Lucy, I want to believe you. But the evidence is right here. I drink white. You drink red." His sweeping gesture encompasses the damning bottles, and his cold tone could freeze water into ice. "We need to face the facts. Maybe you did it without realising. I even found one in the bottom of your wardrobe hidden behind your shoes. Why would you do that?"

Shit. Anger surges through me while I feel my face flush with guilt and embarrassment. I'd been meaning to remove that bottle from the wardrobe and leave it in the boot of my car with the others so I could drop them at the bottle bank in the Tesco's car park, and Greg would have been none the wiser. "Erm. I'm. No," I practically scream, slamming my fist down on the worktop. "I'm not some irresponsible drunk who goes round damaging her own property, misplacing things, staggering round feeling unwell, and seeing imaginary figures out back. Someone is doing this to me, and you won't even entertain the possibility."

Not wanting to see the evidence staring me in the face any longer or listen to Greg's weak attempt at supporting me, I scoop up the bottles and head back out to my car and place them in my boot as Greg follows me.

"Hey, guys. Everything okay?" The concerned voice of our friend Beth cuts through the tension like a knife. She stands at the edge of our driveway, her blue eyes wide with worry.

"Everything's fine, Beth," I snap, trying to force a smile. But she doesn't buy it for a second, her gaze flicking between Greg and me.

"Lucy, I don't want to fight with you." Greg rubs his eyes as he sighs. "But we need to be realistic about this. If you truly believe someone's targeting you, then we should go to the police. But you have to admit, it could just be a case of bad luck or an honest mistake."

"Bad luck? An honest mistake?" I feel my anger surfacing again. "I can't believe you. This isn't just some random string of events. And I don't need you to patronise me."

"I've had enough of this. I'm going inside." Greg storms off, leaving me standing in the driveway with Beth.

"Lucy, what's really going on here?"

"I don't know, but it feels like everything is going wrong. Perhaps I've pissed someone off." My voice breaks as I swipe at my eyes. "And it feels like nobody believes me."

"We're all worried about you," she says. "But sometimes things just go wrong."

"Maybe," I say, unconvinced as I watch Greg disappearing into the house.

"I know you're going through a lot right now," she begins tentatively, staring at the collection of empty wine bottles in my boot, "but maybe it's possible Greg has a point about the drinking? Sometimes one drink can turn into five without us even realising."

Her words sting, making me feel even more vulnerable than before. I clench my fists and bite back the urge to go at her as well. Instead, I take a deep breath and try to explain myself. "Beth, I swear I'm not losing control like that again. I know what it feels like to spiral, and this isn't it."

"Okay, but if it is someone, there must be a reason."

I pause, my mind racing with possibilities. "I don't know who or why, but..." Hesitating, I glance back towards the house. "Ever since Alice arrived, things have changed and got worse."

"That sounds like a coincidence, nothing more. You're just overwhelmed with everything going on in your life. Just remember that I'm here for you and I'll help in whichever way I can." Beth hugs me and I welcome her embrace.

"Thanks," I say reluctantly, but inside, there's a nagging feeling that there's a connection. Why did everything fall apart as soon as Alice entered our lives? It can't just be a random coincidence.

"Hey, we'll get through this, okay?"

As we stand there hugging, I want to believe Beth. But I don't know how much fight I've got left in me.

Beth leaves and I make my way back into the house. The atmosphere inside is heavy with tension, like a thunderstorm waiting to break loose. Greg sits on the sofa, his eyes glued to his phone, seemingly indifferent to the turmoil surrounding him.

"Greg," I begin, working hard to steady my voice. "We need to talk." I wrap my arms round my waist and brace myself.

"About what?" he replies without looking up. His dismissive tone hurts.

"About everything that's been happening and about how I'm feeling. I don't know why, but someone is out to get me."

"Lucy, you can't keep saying that. I really think you need to see the doctor. Talk it through with them. You could get something to help you sleep better?"

"I'm not crazy, Greg. Listen, I've tried to get an appointment to see a doctor. The lines open at eight a.m., and by five past, the slots are all gone. It's a nightmare trying to get through, let alone get an appointment." My voice trembles, anger rising in my chest. Greg's concern feels like an accusation, undermining my already fragile confidence.

"Of course not," he says. "But it's clear that balancing work and being a parent is hard for you. You can't just ignore the signs. You couldn't even hold a knife and fork at the table the other night and kept dropping them, and then when you got up to go to bed, you swayed all over the place like you were blind drunk."

"Is that really all you have to say? You think I'm not coping, and the only solution you have is to get me onto sleeping pills? You shouldn't be so quick to judge," I fire back. "I know what I'm experiencing, and I don't need either of you to tell me how to feel."

"Fine," Greg mutters, throwing his hands up in exasperation. "Do whatever you want. Just don't expect me to stand by and watch you self-destruct. You're impossible sometimes."

"Greg, I—" My words die in my throat, choked off by the rising tide of emotion.

"Lucy, I can't do this right now. Just stop," he says coldly, rising from the sofa to grab the TV remote from the coffee table.

"Fine! But don't you dare follow me!" I shout, storming towards the door. Slamming it behind me, I race down the path, desperate to escape the suffocating feeling. The world round me blurs as I fight to hold back the tears, my chest tightening with every laboured breath.

As I walk, my thoughts swirl like a vortex, each one more destructive than the last. Is Greg right? Am I losing control? Am I being unreasonable? Or is there truly someone pulling at the threads of my life until everything unravels? All I know is that I need answers, and I won't find them at the bottom of a wine glass. I have to uncover the truth. For my sanity, for my family, and for myself.

21

LUCY

As I enter Matthew's bedroom, I shield my eyes from the sharp sunlight filtering through the curtains. The events of last night weigh on my mind. I walked for an hour, wandering aimlessly up and down the quiet streets, trying to clear my head. In my haste, I left wearing only a flimsy cardigan, and by the time Beth found me and persuaded me to come home, I was shivering.

"Lucy, love," she said, wrapping her arm round my shoulders, "you need to go home and sort things out with Greg."

Once home, though, Greg ignored me, staying up late in his study while I struggled to find a comfortable position in bed, feeling more alone than ever. It felt like I was a stranger in my house.

Greg went to the gym early and returned home to work, again keeping to himself in the study. Despite my best efforts when I brought him a cuppa, he barely engaged in conversation. "Greg, please talk to me," I pleaded, but he just mumbled something about having a lot of work to do and closed the door. Deflated, I turned to tidying the house to keep my mind occupied, even though Alice had cleaned the house the day before yesterday for me and would be here any moment to look after the kids.

Now, as I tidy Matthew's room, the heated conversation from last night swims round in my head. My voice sounds strained and frantic and not at all like me.

As I pick up scattered toys and straighten rumpled bedsheets, I feel let down by Greg's lack of support. He's supposed to be my partner, my rock. Instead, he's doubting my sanity and refusing to even listen. But as I stand in the middle of Matthew's room, surrounded by his toys and clothes, a growing sense of helplessness swells within. What if I'm wrong? What if Greg's right, and it's all in my head? What if we get a divorce? They'll stop me from seeing my kids. Worse, they could take my kids away from me. They could see me as a risk to their well-being.

While tidying up Matthew's bedroom, I notice something glinting under his bed. Curious, I reach for it and discover my earrings. I hold them in the palm of my hand, trying to figure out how they could have ended up in Matthew's room. Had Matthew or Sarah taken them to play once I stored them in my jewellery box? Alice cleaned in here. Did she take them and hide them to make it look like Matthew had taken them?

"Lucy?" Greg calls from the study, interrupting my thoughts. "Have you seen my laptop charger?"

"Uh, no, I haven't," I reply, still holding the earrings. The weight of suspicion settles in my chest, but I don't want Greg to know what I've found. Not yet.

"Alright, I'll keep looking," he says.

Entering our bedroom, I notice Greg's gym bag on the floor, out of place from where it normally is. As I push it behind the door, I stop, and narrow my eyes. A ring of mine that I haven't seen for weeks is nestled behind the door. I reach down to pick it up. Has it been here all the time, Greg's bag hiding it from view?

"Lucy?" Alice's voice sounds from behind me, soft and innocent. "Is everything alright?"

I jump, startled by her voice, and turn to face her, clutching the ring in my hand, feeling both fear and anger coursing through my veins. "Have you been hiding or misplacing my things?"

Her eyes widen in shock. "I don't know what you're talking about. I haven't touched your belongings. That would be so inappropriate, and that's the last thing I'd do."

"Then how do you explain my earrings under Matthew's bed after I placed them in my jewellery box, and now my ring on the floor behind the door? You cleaned the house two days ago for me. You would have seen them unless you placed them there after cleaning?"

"I... I don't know, Lucy. Did you misplaced them?"

"Stop playing games with me. Everything was fine until you arrived. I know you're doing this, trying to make me doubt myself. But why? What do you want from me?" Tears sting my eyes as I fist my hands at my sides.

"Lucy, please." She tries to reach out to me, but I back away, glaring at her.

"Stay away from me. I'll find out the truth, and when I do, you won't be able to hide behind your lies any more. I don't want you here any more." I warn her, my voice breaking as I jab a finger towards her.

As I storm out of the room and head downstairs for the lounge, leaving Alice behind, my fingers trail over the gold band of my ring, the cold metal gripped in my palm. Alice's denials echo through my head.

"Lucy? What was the shouting for? What's wrong?" Greg's voice cuts through my thoughts as he enters.

I tap my foot on the floor. "I found my earrings under Matthew's bed, and my ring... it was behind our bedroom door."

Greg's gaze tracks mine. "Maybe the kids were playing with them."

"Since when have the kids *ever* played with my jewellery, they know not to. She's been hiding my things."

He puts a palm out. "Lucy, calm down."

"How can you be so blind? From the moment she arrived, things started going downhill. She's trying to drive me insane, and I don't know why. I want her gone."

"Luce," he sighs, coming towards me and pulling me into his embrace. "I understand you're upset, but accusing Alice with no solid proof will solve nothing. We can't just fire her."

His eyes lock onto mine as he steps back, and for a moment, we stand there as two strangers sharing the same space, a growing chasm of distrust pulling us apart. I shove the ring in his direction. "Then explain why I found my ring behind the door where your bag should be?"

"I don't know. But that doesn't mean Alice did it."

"Doesn't it?" I shout. "She's the only other person in this house! Who else could it be? Are you seriously suggesting I'm doing this to myself?" The words spew out, raw and disbelieving. "That I'm hiding my own things to make Alice look bad? Exactly what would be in that for me?"

"I didn't say that. But if we need to get rid of her then we have to have a valid reason. The agency will want to know and well... she's not done anything wrong. She's not harmed the kids or put them in danger. She's not stolen from us and not been rude towards us."

"Isn't this evidence enough?" My voice rises in pitch.

"How can you trust her when everything points to her being the one pulling strings?"

"Because we need concrete proof. However, we have to contact the agency first to discuss it with them and tell them we've changed our minds. Perhaps this whole nanny thing isn't right for us, and we can come up with another idea so you can continue working? I'll do whatever makes you happy, but we need to be sure, right?"

"Fine." Turning my back on him, I storm back to the dining room to find Alice sitting at the table. Her doe-like eyes widen with innocence as I appear, even though she's heard the argument.

I loom over her. "Have I upset you in any way?"

"Lucy, what you're talking about?"

"Everything was fine before you!" I gesture wildly. "You're the only thing that has changed in this house."

"Lucy, please." Greg steps in, trying to defuse the situation.

"Stay out of it!" I spit, angry at his interference. "This isn't working for us. We don't need you."

"Lucy, we can't do that. Remember what I said. It *needs* to be discussed first."

My head spins with frustration, and my legs wobble beneath me.

"Luce." Greg catches me before I hit the ground, guiding me into a chair. "Take a deep breath, darling. You're okay."

"Stop trying to control me!" The room spinning doesn't stop me from shouting. Because I feel like I'm screaming into a void. No one listens. No one cares.

"Try to have some water and something to eat," he suggests as he strokes my face. "You might feel better."

I nod, reluctant to admit that he might be right as my

tummy growls and my mouth dries up. As if on cue, Alice scurries off to the kitchen.

Later, we sit round the dinner table, the tension palpable. Alice refuses our offer to join us as she entertains the kids upstairs. Disappointment washes over my husband, and I don't even register his presence. As the evening wears on, my determination grows. I will uncover Alice's deception, and when I do, Greg will have to believe me. No matter what it takes, I'll expose Alice for the manipulative liar she is. The silence between Greg and me deepens, broken only by the distant sound of Alice coming downstairs.

"Lucy," Alice's eyes soften as she purses her lips, "I wanted to say how sorry I am about all this. I know how you must be feeling about me."

"Right." The word comes out sharp.

"Perhaps I can help you look round the house for anything else that might be misplaced?" At her gentle and sincere tone—the one I'm now sure she's perfected as part of her twisted game—it takes all my self-control not to roll my eyes at her feigned kindness, punch her in the face and drag her to the front door. "Thanks, but I'm okay." I force a smile, my voice dripping with sarcasm. "I wouldn't want you to have to go through any more trouble on my account."

"Are you sure, Luce?" Greg says.

I turn my head and spear my husband with a lethal glare. "Really? You think I need help? I can look after myself and my own belongings. Please don't take it personally, Alice, but I need space right now."

"Of course." She nods, leaving to grab her coat and bag. "Let me know if you change your mind."

The light of our big lamp in the lounge casts long shadows on the walls. I sit on the couch, my fingers fidgeting in my lap as Greg remains standing, arms crossed, his hazel eyes narrowed with scepticism. I try to reason with Greg, plead with him, but he's not listening. There's something off about that woman. However, my words go unheard as Greg repeats the same thing over and over. She's trying to manipulate us. But no one else can see it.

If Greg won't listen, I'll have to prove it myself. But I'm not sure how. I will uncover the truth about Alice, and I will protect the people I love, no matter what it takes.

22

ALICE

The room is dark and gloomy, like my mood. Just a small table lamp casts its glow on the wall in front of me. Though I have the window wide open, the atmosphere feels crushing, heavy with the weight of memories that seem to hang from every wall. With my back pressed against the closed door and my arms folded across my chest to protect me, my eyes dance across the newspaper clippings pinned to the wall like a disjointed tapestry of misery. Each one tells a story, some distant and cold, others so painful they cut through me like an ice-cold sword.

My eyes linger on the familiar faces that have haunted my dreams for years. The tears well up and tumble down my cheeks, blurring the words and images until they merge into an indistinguishable mass. "Bloody hell," I mutter, wiping at my cheeks.

TRAGIC ACCIDENT reads the headline of one clipping, accompanied by a black-and-white photo of twisted plastic and shattered glass. And then there's the other picture, the one that shows Jordan smiling and carefree, forever frozen in time.

"Look at you." Stepping forward, I trace the outline of his face with a trembling finger. "You deserved better, didn't you?"

The silence which follows is both comforting and oppressive, filling the void left behind by Jordan's absence. My brother. The brother I looked up to. My breath catches as I force myself to focus, to channel the pain and anger that has overwhelmed me for far too long.

"Can't let them win," I say.

I find myself drawn to another image, one that fills me with equal parts envy and hatred. Lucy, her face radiant with happiness as she goes about her daily life, unaware of me as I lurk in the shadows, watching her every move. I see her laughing with Beth, playing with Matthew and Sarah, holding Greg close as if he's her lifeline as they stand in the park watching their kids play.

"Lucy." I spit the name out like I've sucked on a lemon slice, clenching my fists until my nails dig into the soft flesh of my palms. "You'll pay for what you've done. I swear it."

As each day passes, it's getting harder. Lucy and I are at odds with each other, Greg an unlikely intermediary trying to keep the peace.

Patience. It's all about timing. I'm so close. She won't get away with what she did. A breeze rushes in and makes the newspaper clippings on my wall rustle, and it's as if my brother is right here with me, urging me forward, listening to everything. My gaze shifts towards the window. I know he's here. I can feel his presence.

"Tell me what to do, Jordan," I say, pacing the room. "How can I make her pay?"

As I walk, my conversation continues between me and

my brother. He's talking to me. I can hear his voice. It's as if he's guiding me, his spirit still protecting me from the grave.

"Stay focused, Alice," Jordan says. "Don't let your emotions get in the way. She's fighting back. Don't let her."

"Right," I say, determined. "I am focused, Jordan. I'll watch her closely. I'll break her down."

"Good," Jordan's voice echoes in my head. "And remember that I'm always with you, even if you can't see me. I'm right by your side. We're in this together. I've seen what you've done so far. It's been ace. The zopiclone was a nice touch. See if you can give her more. It will send her right off the rails."

"Yeah," I say excitedly.

My heart aches at the thought of my brother, but I find comfort in knowing that he's by my side, and that together we'll bring Lucy down and give Jordan the justice he deserves.

"Thank you, Jordan," I murmur, wiping away a stray tear. "I won't let you down. I promise. I'll see you soon." I take a moment to steady myself. But the sight of her smiling face, so full of warmth and charm, it's too much. The anger surges within me, uncontrollable and fierce. Before I can even think, my fist flies towards the wall with a sickening crunch. "Shit," I growl, as pain shoots through my fingers.

"Careful, Alice. You need to keep it together," Jordan warns me.

"Sorry, Jordan," I apologise. "I'll try."

"I'm waiting for you, Alice," he says as his voice fades.

23

LUCY

THE DOORBELL RINGS and I roll my eyes. Greg gave me fair warning, and there she is, his mum, Diane, standing on our doorstep with a wide grin plastered across her smug face. "Hello, Lucy dear. I couldn't sleep because I was so excited, so I thought I'd get here a bit early to watch the kids today since it's Alice's day off."

"Thanks, Diane," I say with a thin smile, trying my best to sound thankful. As much as I'm grateful for her help, I can't stand her interference. She's always calling Greg with advice on how to manage the kids, and it makes me feel like I'm not doing enough. But I can't show that side of me now, not when she's here to lend a hand.

"Come on in." I stand to one side. Thankfully, I convinced Greg a long time ago to not give his mum a key to our place. Given half the chance, she'd be here every other day sticking her nose in everything that goes on under this roof. Our kids, our marriage, the cooking, cleaning, gardening, and everything in between.

The moment Diane steps foot into the house, she

gushes over the children. Her arms wrap round them, smothering them with hugs and kisses like she hasn't seen them in months. "My babies this, my babies that..." They squirm and giggle, but I know they're as uncomfortable as I am. And yet, despite my annoyance, I hold my tongue, reminding myself that Diane means well.

"Okay, you lot," Diane announces, finally releasing the kids from her vice-like grip. "Why don't you go play upstairs while I chat with your mum?"

I glance at the clock, feeling the pressure of time eating into my day. I need to leave for work soon, but I still haven't finished getting ready. As the kids disappear upstairs, I turn to Diane.

"You don't need to stay the whole afternoon. I'll be back before you know it. An hour or two max."

"Lucy, dear, don't worry about it," she replies, her tone sickly sweet. "I know you have a lot going on, and I'm more than happy to lend a hand. I wish you'd let me come over more."

"Thank you." The words don't come easy, but I force them out anyway. It's true that I need the help. As I dash round the lounge trying to gather my things for work, Diane continues to hover, trailing me. She watches me like a hawk, and I feel judged, as if every move I make is being scrutinised against a mental checklist. I try to ignore her, focusing instead on my breathing, but it's impossible to shake the feeling of her eyes boring into my back.

"Lucy," she calls out, making me jump.

"Y-yes?" I stammer, fumbling with my handbag.

"You seem a bit... frazzled?"

"Diane, I'm fine," I say with a smile as I dash back into the kitchen. "I'm in a hurry, that's all."

"Alright, if you say so." Not sounding convinced, she

pauses for a moment, still studying me. "You look peaky, though. Are you sure you're okay?"

"Of course, I'm fine." My voice is tainted with irritation, but I force myself to soften my tone. "In fact, I'm pleased to be working again. It's been... a lot, you know?"

Diane nods, but her eyes stay watchful. "I understand. Just remember to take care of yourself, too. You can't help anyone else if you're running on empty."

I watch Diane's movements, her fingers sliding across the kitchen worktop as if searching for some dust or food crumbs. "Lucy, I'm worried about you taking on too much." My mother-in-law's eyes fix on my face. "I'm more than happy to help babysit Matthew and Sarah. I have so much free time now that I'm retired."

"Thank you, but..." I try to butt in, but she ploughs on like she always does when I try to talk.

"I've been thinking... I can stay here a few days a week? You have a spare room, and I can look after the children and tidy the house." Her gaze flickers round the kitchen, lingering on a biscuit crumb she's discovered. "I don't understand why you'd want a nanny when I'm right here willing to help. It would be much better for the kids, don't you think?"

My body stiffens, and I bite down hard on my tongue to stop a sharp reply from escaping. Greg's mum was never happy about her son marrying me and she made a point of it by dropping Caroline's name in many conversations after Greg and I first started dating. She even called me Caroline on a few occasions, laughing it off as a Freudian slip. She had always envisioned him with Caroline Archer, a big shot city lawyer who followed in the footsteps of both her barrister parents before they took early retirement and travelled the world.

"You know, Lucy," God, the woman's voice sounds like nails on a blackboard, "I have the number of a cleaning company. They could knock this house into shape in an afternoon. It could certainly do with a deep clean." Her eyes flicker over the kitchen floor, my stomach churning at her judgement.

"Really?" I say, losing control of my emotions for a moment. "We don't need the extra help."

Her eyes widen. "But..."

"Thank you for the offer," I say through gritted teeth. "But we have everything under control."

"But you're stretched," she stresses, reaching out to touch my arm. I pull away, trying to hide my irritation. "You need family to help you, not a random person off the street."

Her words bounce round in my head, and anger stiffens my shoulders, but I must hold back. I don't think Greg would appreciate his mother with a black eye no matter how good it might feel to deck her.

"We're good." The edge in my voice betrays my rising emotion. "We've got it covered. I appreciate your concern, but we're managing fine."

"Alright then," she replies with a sigh, her eyes narrowing as if she doesn't quite believe me. "If you change your mind, you know where to find me."

"Of course," I say. "Thank you for watching the kids today. I need to head off to work."

"Take care." As she watches me, Diane's tone is laced with something that feels less like genuine concern and more like condescension.

I turn away from her, grabbing my bag and making my way to the door. With each step, I can feel the weight of her gaze on me, scrutinising my every move.

"Lucy," Diane calls after me as I yank the door open, her voice sharp and disapproving. I pause for a moment, my back still turned to her, the fresh air outside a welcome reprieve from the stuffy atmosphere inside.

"Bye," I reply, forcing a sense of calm I don't feel.

24

LUCY

The air in the room feels stuffy as I sit at the long mahogany table surrounded by my team and manager. A thirty-minute meeting has turned into ninety minutes so far as Brad rants on about rising costs and delays to deliveries. My phone lights up on the table beside me, but I ignore it, determined to stay focused on the meeting. Another call comes in, and I see the familiar voicemail icon showing a message has been left. I take a peek at the screen, but I don't recognise the number.

Seconds later, Greg's number flashes on the screen. I ignore it again, trying to keep my composure amidst the tense discussion round me about next year's spring/summer collection and what we've secured so far. But when his name appears for the second time, my heart leaps into my throat, and I can't ignore it any longer. I excuse myself from the meeting and step out into the hallway. I feel Brad's eyes burn into the back of my head as the door closes behind me.

"Greg, what's up? I'm in the middle of a meeting."

"Lucy." His calm tone belies the urgency of the situation. "Matthew's been in an accident at home, and he's been taken to hospital."

My legs go weak, and I can barely breathe as I dash back into the meeting room to grab my bag. My team looks on in consternation and shock as I excuse myself. "I'm really sorry, Brad, but my son has been hurt and is on the way to the hospital. I've got to go."

Though Brad looks annoyed at being interrupted in mid flow, I sense his concern as he leans into the table.

"Oh, that's not good to hear. You go. I hope he's okay."

I thank Brad and leave in a hurry. Images of Matthew, our little boy, flash through my mind. His laughter, his bright eyes that mirror my own. The thought of him injured crushes my chest.

After racing through the streets at breakneck speed, I burst through the doors of A & E, scanning the chaotic scene for Greg. As if sensing my presence, he turns and locks eyes with me, his face a mask of concern. I rush to his side, desperate for answers.

"What happened?" I demand, my voice trembling.

"One of Sarah's tantrums distracted Mum in the lounge after Matthew wound her up. Mum went after Matthew as he ran from the room with one of Sarah's dolls. But then Mum thought she heard the kitchen door to the garden open, so she went to have a look and in just the space of a few seconds, Matthew raced up the stairs to get away and slipped back down, injuring himself. Mum called for an ambulance." He pauses for a moment, catching my gaze before adding, "He's got a few cuts, bruises to his face and chest, and they think he has a concussion from where he hit his head on the wall coming down. It was a nasty fall, at least seven or eight steps."

My heart clenches with relief, but it's short-lived as I

process the details. Diane, Greg's mother, was responsible for our children while I was at work. How could she let this happen? But there's no time to dwell on that now. Matthew needs me.

As we make our way to the cubicle, Alice, our nanny, appears out of nowhere. She spots us and hurries over. Her sudden appearance catches me off guard, but I'm too stressed to question it.

"Lucy, Greg, I came as soon as Greg called." Her brown eyes reflect her concern. "I'm here to help. What can I do?"

"Thank you, Alice," Greg replies, his voice soft and genuine. "I need you to watch Sarah for a bit, please."

Alice nods and takes charge of soothing Sarah while Greg and I sit with Matthew in a sterile cubicle that smells of disinfectant... and coffee for some reason. These cubicles function like a merry-go-round for the sick and unwell. The medical staff assess them here before dispatching them to various parts of the hospital. Matthew looks so small and vulnerable in the large hospital bed, his face pale and sporting a swollen lip, grazed cheek, and nose. I reach out and take his hand in mine.

"Matthew, sweetheart, Mummy's here. We'll be going home soon." As I stare down at my injured child, I fight back tears.

My boy responds with a weak smile, and I squeeze his hand. But as I sit surrounded by the chaos of the hospital, I can't dislodge the thought this is another incident our family has suffered in such a short space of time.

Greg slides the key into the front door of our home, and we step inside tired and exhausted. I wait for Greg to carry Matthew upstairs to bed before I usher a sleepy Sarah to her bedroom and get her ready for an early night too. The events of today have taken their toll on all of us. Diane wanted to follow us over from the hospital, but the mere sight of the older woman flared my anger, and before Greg replied, I brushed her off and told her we could manage fine.

"I can't believe this happened. I know your mum would love to help more, and that's kind of her, but maybe it's too much for her? The kids can be a handful at the best of times... even for us," I say, as he appears in the dining room where I'm sitting with my head in my hands. "Matthew could have been seriously hurt. What if it had been worse?"

Greg runs his fingers through his hair and sighs. "Lucy, it's not just about my mum. It could have happened to any one of us. Mum's out of practice a bit, that's all. You know how hard it is to keep up with our son. It's a one-off incident."

"Everything is going wrong now. Can't you see it? My car getting damaged, my jewellery being hidden, someone watching the back of our house at night, back doors being left open, and now Matthew falling down the stairs when your mum should have been watching him. Everything was fine before..." I glance up at Greg.

"Yes, and everything was fine. But you've started drinking again and that doesn't help."

His words sting, and I feel as if he's slapped me across the face. I struggle to control the anger that flares up inside me. "What do you mean? Are you blaming me for everything that's been happening? Are you saying that I imagined seeing someone watching the house?" With each frantic question, my voice rises in pitch.

"Not at all, sweetheart. I don't deny that odd things have been happening recently and I don't know why, but trying to find the answer at the bottom of a bottle doesn't help you or me. I want answers as much as you do but your reaction to these events worries me."

As he speaks, I think about the mounting pressure I've felt since returning to work. The sleepless nights, the endless to-do lists, the constant sensation of being pulled in a hundred different directions. I clench my fists, trying to suppress the overwhelming emotions stirring within me. "I guess you're right, Greg," I admit. "Perhaps I haven't been able to handle everything as well as I thought."

"I want us to work together to figure out what's best for our family," Greg says.

I nod, blinking back tears. He's right, we need to find a solution, for the sake of our children.

"Was the door open?" I ask as I narrow my eyes, my mind whirring.

My husband looks puzzled. "Sorry?"

I point toward it. "The kitchen door. Was it open?"

He lifts one shoulder and lets it drop. "I don't know. I didn't check with Mum."

But even as we discuss our situation, a dark suspicion continues to gnaw at me, making me question everything I once believed about our perfect life. And I wonder if the person responsible for my growing sense of unease is closer than I think.

The image of Matthew on that hospital bed flashes before my eyes. "Greg, this is Alice's fault," I blurt out, my voice laced with a mix of anger and frustration. "She was supposed to watch Sarah, and instead, she created distractions that led to Matthew's accident."

"Lucy," Greg pauses briefly before continuing, "you're not thinking straight. Alice wasn't even there when it happened. She arrived later, remember? I called her to ask for her help with Sarah. You can't blame her for this."

"Fine. But something is wrong here, and I need answers." I avert my gaze to the tabletop, unable to meet his gaze.

He heaves a tired sigh. "Look, we're both tired and stressed. Let's think about this tomorrow. You need some sleep, sweetheart."

The sound of the front doorbell stops us both in our tracks as Greg goes to answer it. Beth follows Greg into the dining room, concern etched on her face as she takes in the sight of Greg and me, glaring at each other.

"Hey, I got your text, Lucy," she says. "Is everything okay? Is Matthew okay?"

"Fine," I mutter, as I glare at Greg.

"Okay. Not a good time. I think I should go," Beth offers, sensing the tension in the air.

"No. Stay. Please," I blurt out.

"Lucy—" Greg protests, but I cut him off.

"Please, Greg, let's not do this in front of Beth," I say.

He gives a single nod and steps away from the confrontation. "Alright, I'll be upstairs if you need me. But please don't stay up too late."

As soon as he's out of earshot, I drop my head and hide my face in my hands.

"What's going on?" Beth asks, sitting down beside me.

"Everything's... falling apart," I admit, tears streaming down my cheeks. "Matthew's accident today, this fight with Greg... I don't know what's happening to us."

"Hey, it's going to be alright," she reassures me, rubbing my back. "You're going through a rough patch. It happens to the best of us."

I struggle not to break down completely. "Does it? Or am I failing as a mother, as a wife?"

"You are not a failure. But maybe... maybe get some advice. Speak to someone."

"Advice?" I say, my pride wounded. "You mean like therapy?"

She shrugs. "Or someone to talk to, like a working mum's support group. It might help you sort through all this stress and figure out how to handle it better. You want to work, and you want to make sure the kids are okay, and you need to keep a house running. So, what are other mums doing to juggle all those balls? They might have some great advice or tips?"

My head snaps up. "Greg put you up to this, didn't he?"

"No, I promise. This is me, your friend, trying to help. I hate seeing you like this. You deserve to be happy, and if getting help or advice can give you that, then why not try?"

I consider her words. Is this what it has reduced me to? Needing help to get through the chaos of my life? "I'll think about it."

"Good." Beth smiles, relief washing over her face. "Remember, we're all here for you, Luce. You don't have to go through this alone."

"Someone's trying to make me look bad." The familiar sensation of paranoia creeps into my mind. "Ever since I went back to work, it's like there's a target on my back."

"You're just stressed and exhausted. It's not about someone being out to get you," Beth pleads. I flinch away from her touch, feeling exposed and vulnerable.

"Isn't it, though? Nothing feels right any more. And today, with Matthew... it's like everything's falling apart."

"Lucy..." Beth trails off, unsure of what to say.

"Maybe I'm not handling things too well," I concede, the pressure of the past few weeks perhaps getting to me. "Maybe I'm so caught up in this whirlwind of stress and paranoia that I don't know which way is up any more."

As Beth continues to speak, I want to believe her. But what choice do I have? In a world where nothing makes sense any more, where every move feels like it could be my last, what else can I do but hold on tight to the people I love and hope they don't betray me?

25

LUCY

I'M SHATTERED, every fibre of my being aching from the day's endless stress. With Matthew asleep and Beth gone, I feel a small sense of relief as I walk out to the car. The cold air prickles my skin, but I need to fetch my work bag and laptop from the boot.

My hand is on the boot release when a noise startles me. I glance over my shoulder and see it, a dark figure ducking behind a tree. My eyes widen as a wave of icy fear washes over me. I race back to the house and stop and turn in the doorway. Gasping for breath, I look round for any movement. The street appears empty, not even a cat or fox mooching from one garden to another. Could exhaustion be playing tricks on me? I guess I imagined it.

My hands shake as I hold my phone, ready to capture any movement on camera. Before I can convince myself that it is all in my head, the figure darts out from behind a parked car a few houses away, and stares at me, their face hidden in the darkness of a hoodie, before running off down the street. A choked scream escapes my lips as it vanishes into the darkness, my phone capturing the last seconds of movement.

"Oi," I shout. But they've disappeared.

"Greg. Greg, come quick," I shout, my voice cracking with fear.

He rushes towards me from upstairs. "What's the matter?"

"Someone was outside, watching me." I jab my finger down the road, words tumbling from my lips. "They ran off when they spotted me. Look, I took these outside." I show him the images on the screen as we stop in the doorway.

He takes the phone and studies the photos, his eyes narrowing in concentration.

"I don't see anyone in these pictures. It looks like it's the trees, cars, and shadows." He hands me back my phone.

I snatch it from him. "No, there was someone there, Greg. I'm not imagining things."

"Alright, stay here." He grabs his coat and steps out into the night air.

"Be careful," I call after him, my heart pounding.

Minutes feel like hours as I wait for Greg to return. When he reappears, I feel relieved. "Did you spot anything?"

"Nothing. There's no one lurking," he says, trying to sound reassuring.

Staring outside, I grimace. "I know I saw something."

"Alright, I'll take another look. You stay here to listen out for the kids." He grabs the torch from the hallway table and heads back out into the darkness.

With each step, he scans the gardens, parked cars, and the trees, searching for any movement, but there's nothing. My mind races with questions and doubts, while Greg wanders round the street.

"There's no one around. Whoever it was, they've gone." When he returns, he seems a bit stressed.

"Maybe they're hiding," I argue, knowing I sound irrational but unable to stop myself.

He breathes out a weary sigh, running a hand down his face. "Alright, let's say there was someone. What do you want to do about it? I've searched the area and found nothing."

As I close the door, the creepy feeling lingers.

"Are you alright?" Greg asks, his voice softer now as he notices my discomfort.

His question hangs in the air, and for a moment, I hesitate, feeling vulnerable and exposed. "I'm scared," I admit, my voice barely above a whisper, each word trembling with a mix of fear and frustration, echoing the turmoil churning inside me.

My husband's constant scepticism presses down on me like a physical burden, his dismissive attitude eroding the last remnants of my strength. Each dubious look, every doubting word, feels like a dismissal not just of my concerns but of me, leaving me isolated in my own fears, struggling under the heavy cloak of his lack of faith.

"Come here." He pulls me into a tight hug for a few moments. I welcome the gesture before he checks the doors are locked and he heads upstairs to bed.

As soon as I hear the bedroom light click off, I grab my laptop and begin searching for ways to protect my family. I will not sit idly by while someone terrorises us. My gut feeling tells me that Alice has something to do with it. All these strange and unsettling events have happened since she arrived. I'm convinced she's hiding something beneath her quiet, harmless exterior.

I really need a glass of wine to calm my nerves, but Greg's been on at me for days now about my drinking, so it takes every ounce of willpower not to head to the larder to sneak a glass. As I close my laptop, the exhaustion that's been building up crashes over me like a tidal wave, dragging me down as I make my way to join Greg. As I sit on the edge of the bed in the darkness, with Greg's shallow snoring, I feel overwhelmed by the constant suspicions floating round in my mind. The thought of Alice being behind this seems ludicrous, but I can't ignore my instincts.

Wondering if it's even possible, I try to piece together why Alice would do this. Would she want something from us? Is she after Greg? They get on well, but there's nothing to suggest anything else. Perhaps she wants me out of the way?

"Lucy, please go to sleep," Greg rolls over and murmurs from behind me, his voice groggy. He reaches for my waist and pulls me in close to him.

"Sorry, I didn't mean to wake you."

My heart races as I imagine all the different scenarios that could unfold if Alice is behind this. But until I have proof, I won't confront her. I can't risk causing more chaos in our already strained household. I'll keep an eye on Alice. As I lay beside Greg, listening to his steady breathing again, I let out a sigh as I close my eyes.

26

ALICE

I watch from the shadows as Beth steps from her house and makes her way to Lucy's in a hurry. Greg opens the door and gives Beth a kiss on the cheek before closing the door behind her. I clench my fists in frustration. Beth is always round, making it difficult for me to get Lucy alone. If only she could stay away.

As I continue to watch, I grow more determined than ever to hurt Lucy. But the drugs aren't working. I've noticed she hasn't touched a drop of wine in days, in part due to Greg giving her a hard time about her drinking. *Thanks, Greg!* She's becoming stronger, more confrontational, and it's getting harder to manipulate her. Every time she lashes out, my heart breaks a little more. If I can make her more unstable, more dependent on me, perhaps I can get back control. Maybe I could spike her tea, but she's becoming more suspicious of me and anything and everything I do. Time is running out for me. If Lucy gets her way, I could get my marching orders any day now.

"Alright, I'll see you tomorrow," Beth calls out after what feels like an eternity. She hugs Lucy goodbye and heads back to her house, leaving Lucy standing on her doorstep.

My eyes narrow as I make my plans. The next time I'm able to get close to her, I'll lace her drink with twice as much zopiclone as before, ensuring she becomes even more reliant on me. It's risky, but it's the only way to make sure I stay employed with the Butlers. I know she's not had much wine recently and she likes tea occasionally, so perhaps I can slip some into her cup the next time she has one.

Lucy steps out of her house and approaches her car as I watch from behind a tree. I need to get closer to her car and hope she doesn't loiter too long. But a cat leaps from a nearby garden wall onto a bin lid, making a loud thud that startles both Lucy and me.

"Who's there?" Lucy calls out. Has she heard or seen something? I can't tell, but the fear in her eyes tells me she's worried. I step further into the shadows, hoping to stay hidden.

"Greg!" she screams, darting back into the house. Panic rises in my chest as I realise I need to leave before Greg comes to the door.

Blindly, I sprint towards the end of the street, my pulse pounding in my head. Lucy's shouts echo in the distance, but I can't afford to look back. Racing towards my car, I fumble with the keys, struggling to unlock the door. My hands shake, but the door clicks open, and I leap inside, slamming it shut behind me. Before pulling away, I check the rear-view mirror, scanning for any sign of Greg or Lucy. They're nowhere to be seen.

I put the car into gear and drive off into the darkness, my mind racing with thoughts of what could have happened if they caught me. Tonight is a failure, but it's only a temporary setback. I'll get closer to Lucy and when the time is right, I'll make my move. The streets are empty, so I need to drive carefully and not draw attention to myself.

"Shit, why did Lucy come out at that exact moment?" I growl, slapping the steering wheel. "So close." My plan to sabotage her car was perfect. A tiny cut in one of the brake pipes would lead to a slow leak of fluid, causing sudden brake failure when she least expected it. An accident waiting to happen.

I try to regain control of my galloping thoughts. What's the next move? Jordan's advice comes back to me, his words echoing in my head like a twisted and sick mantra. "Twice as much zopiclone."

Yes, that's what I'll do. When I'm next there, I'll make sure I spike her drink with even more of the sedative. It's a matter of finding the right opportunity and catching Lucy off guard again. "Lucy, you won't know what hit you," I say above the hum of the engine. A smile tugs at the corners of my mouth as I imagine the effect it will have on her. Patience, I remind myself, my fingers drumming on the wheel.

Breaking Lucy is all I can think about as another idea forms in my mind and I'll need Greg for this one. "Enjoy your peace while it lasts," I say into the night, the darkness swallowing my words. "Because I won't rest until you're broken."

27

LUCY

My body aches this morning as I load the kids into the car. I try to stay upbeat and hide the avalanche of negativity that weighs on my mind like an invisible cloak despite the events of the past few days. I need to get them out of the house for a bit, give them a break from the stifling atmosphere that's settled over us. Though Matthew is still sore and shaken up, he's been resting is bed for days and is fed up.

"Right, guys," I say, "how about we treat ourselves to McDonald's? And then we can go for a long drive as we head home?"

Matthew nods, his face lighting up with excitement. I know he's in pain and he's not his normal self today. "Can I have a Happy Meal?" he says through swollen lips.

I smile. "Of course, sweetheart."

Sarah chimes in too, trying her best to look cheerful for her brother's sake. The resilience of children never ceases to amaze me. How can they bounce back so quickly when I feel like I'm being crushed under the weight of it all? We drive towards the McDonald's near Cambridge city airport, a quick journey that takes us through quiet, leafy streets before hitting the busy A3103. It's a beautiful day, but I can't bring myself to enjoy it. My thoughts are a whirlwind of fear and confusion, playing tug of war with my emotions.

"Are we nearly there, Mum?" Matthew asks, breaking into my reverie.

"Almost, darling," I reply. The sight of their innocent faces in the rear-view mirror tugs at my heartstrings. They deserve better than this. And so do I. "We have to take a detour because there are roadworks ahead. Shouldn't be too long now."

As we pull into the car park, I'm ready to face the world. We're going to grab a quick meal, nothing more. I can handle that. The kids unbuckle their seat belts and clamber out, their eyes shining with anticipation.

"Come on, Mum," Sarah urges, grabbing my hand and pulling me towards the entrance.

"Alright, alright." A rare burst of laughter escapes my lips. For the first time in days, I feel a glimmer of hope. Maybe we can get through this together and everything will be okay.

With tummies full and hunger satisfied, we make our way back, taking a different route to the one we took earlier. It's not an area of Cambridge I'm too familiar with, so it's a pleasant distraction as I point out various things to the kids.

"Only a few more minutes, kids," I say as we approach the traffic lights. We wait for our turn to cross the busy road.

My gaze drifts across the street, and time seems to freeze. A frigid shock courses through me, rattling me to my core. There's Greg, casually meeting Alice outside a coffee shop on her day off. They're laughing together, their ease with each other unnatural, too intimate. Then Greg, with a familiarity that sears my soul, places his hand on the small of Alice's back, guiding her through the door.

I knew it. I fucking knew it!

A cold, leaden dread drops like a stone in my stomach, and bile claws its way up my throat, leaving a bitter, acidic burn. This scene unfolding before my eyes—it's a visceral punch to the gut, a nightmare turned into reality. With waves of nausea threatening, the steering wheel slips through my fingers and I have to right the vehicle before I drive off the road.

"Are you okay, Mum?" Matthew asks, his voice enquiring. The car horn behind us blares, jolting me from my daze. I swallow down the urge to retch, forcing a smile onto my face.

"Fine, sweetheart. I'm stuffed after all those fries, that's all," I lie as my heart thunders inside of me.

The rest of the journey passes in a blur. I plaster a smile on my face, trying to ignore the mixture of feelings and the tide of questions threatening to drown me. Why was he meeting her? Why didn't Greg mention it? Are they in this together? Has she got to him? Is Greg having an affair with *our* nanny? I can't make sense of this. A part of me wants to pull over so I can get out of the car and scream. The other part wants to crawl under the duvet and cry.

I stumble through the door, watching Matthew and Sarah natter away as they kick off their shoes. They're still buzzing from their trip to McDonald's—a rare treat for all of us. I smile at their joy, even if only for a moment, before the image of Greg and Alice together earlier today comes crashing back into my mind.

"Go on, you two, get cleaned up," I tell them, trying to

keep my voice steady. "We don't want greasy fingers all over the place, do we?"

"Okay, Mum," Sarah squeals, hopping up the stairs, with Matthew following slowly behind, his body sore and stiff from his fall. Their laughter is infectious and so pure, and I almost forget about what I saw. Almost.

As soon as they're out of sight, my eyes widen and my hands tremble again, the memory of Greg and Alice in town causing my breath to come in ragged gasps. How could he? The question echoes in my head, as moments of despair give way to flashes of anger.

I push to take deep breaths, pushing the thoughts aside. My focus is on caring for my kids, not on whatever might go on behind my back. I'll handle that later when they're asleep and I can confront Greg, although I'm not sure what I'll say. "Oh, hi Greg, are you shagging Alice behind my back?"

"Did you have fun, Mum?" Matthew calls from the bathroom, jolting me back to reality.

"Of course, sweetie." I swallow hard. "I always enjoy spending time with you and your sister."

The running water muffles his tiny voice. "I wish we could do this every day."

"Well, maybe not every day, Matthew, but we'll do it more often, I promise."

"Yay!" both Matthew and Sarah cheer. For now, that's all that matters. I can't let my own fear and anger take away from their joy.

Matthew's eyes grow heavy with sleep, and I can tell he's exhausted. "Alright, little man. Let's get you to bed. You can have a little nap. I'm sure you're tired and a little sore from your fall."

"Okay, Mum." He doesn't protest, and it's clear he's ready for a bit of rest too.

"Sarah, while your brother has a little nap, why don't you play in your room for a bit?"

My daughter's already grabbing her favourite toys that lay on the landing in a pile ready to go downstairs and skips off to her bedroom.

As I tuck Matthew in and kiss him on the forehead, I feel the weight of my earlier discovery settling back onto my chest. But now is not the time to dwell on it. I need to stay busy and keep my mind occupied until Greg comes home. Then, we'll talk.

I head to our bedroom, where the laundry basket is almost overflowing. The scent of Greg's unwashed gym clothes lingers in the air, making me cringe. I can't put this unpleasant task off any longer. "Right, let's get this sorted then," I mutter under my breath, trying to focus on my chores rather than the dark thoughts inside me. I separate the lights from the darks, deciding to tackle the bigger pile first. One by one, I check each item before tossing it into a laundry bag to bring downstairs. My fingers brush against Greg's still sweaty gym T-shirt, and the smell makes me gag. How could I have let it sit here for so long?

"Ugh, disgusting," I groan, feeling like I'll catch something from the T-shirt as I pinch it between two fingers. Why didn't I wash it sooner? It's another thing to add to the growing list of bothersome things between Greg and me. He's a grown adult and can take care of his own washing instead of leaving everything to me. But even as I continue sorting through the laundry, I can't get rid of the image of my husband and Alice together, laughing and chatting like old friends, or perhaps something more.

The persistent doubt and suspicion eat away at me, making it impossible to concentrate on even the most mundane task of washing clothes. It's as if my entire world is teetering on the edge, waiting for one last shove to send it spiralling into chaos, and everything feels like it's out of my grasp. And I wonder if will I be strong enough to pick up the pieces when it all comes crashing down round my ears?

My hand moves to the next item in the pile, Greg's jeans. As I reach into his pockets to double-check again, my fingers brush against something unfamiliar. My heart in my throat, I tug out a small, square packet. A condom. I freeze, my breath trapped inside my burning lungs as I look at the object in my hand. Is this real? Are my eyes playing tricks on me? Has the stress of the last few weeks taken its toll, pushing me to imagine things that aren't there? I close my eyes for a few seconds and open them, hoping that I'm holding a piece of paper or a sweet wrapper.

Greg... no. I don't dare speak the words aloud. But here is the evidence that threatens to undermine everything I believed about my husband and about us. Why would he do this to me? To our family? Desperation claws at my chest, fighting for an explanation that might somehow make sense. But my mind comes up with a big fat zero, only more questions and doubts. I stagger back, collapsing onto the edge of our bed. My stomach somersaults, bile stinging the back of my throat as if I'm about to throw up all the hurt and betrayal that's threatening to drown me.

The evidence is there in my fingers, mocking me. It crushes my chest as if I'm gripped in between an invisible vice until I can't breathe. The condom packet slips from my trembling fingers, falling to the floor as if it were a red-hot iron poker that I can't hold any longer. I can't look away from it while I wrestle to process what I've found.

A voice in my head demands that I confront him as soon as he comes home this evening to get answers and fight for the truth. But another part of me shrinks back, terrified of what those answers might be, and whether they'll destroy us and my family beyond repair. As I sit there on the edge of the bed, caught in this agonising limbo between wanting to know and fearing the truth, I wonder if our marriage can survive this storm. Or will we be swept away by the torrent of lies that seem to grow stronger with each passing day?

28

ALICE

With Diane's unexpected appearance at the Butlers' lingering in my thoughts, a sense of urgency prickles at me. If she's stepping in more, I need to speed up my plans. I shove these thoughts to the side, my body tense with impatience as I reach for my phone. Dialling Greg's number feels like igniting a fuse, and I wait, the phone pressed against my ear, as it rings.

"Hi, Greg, it's Alice. There's something I need to talk to you about." I deliberately sound concerned, my tone carefully crafted to snag his attention.

His voice comes through, questioning yet unaware of the web I'm weaving. "Hi, Alice. What's up? Is everything okay?"

I smile, the thrill of manipulation a sweet taste on my tongue. "I'd rather talk to you in person if that's okay. Can we meet for a quick coffee?"

"Of course. I'm busy now, but I can meet you at Benji's café in town in an hour."

The satisfaction blooms inside me, almost manic in its intensity. "That would be great. Thank you, Greg. See you soon." As I end the call, a wild, unbalanced energy courses through me, a predator setting the stage for her next move.

Now I have to prepare myself for the meeting, knowing Greg is vital for my plan to succeed. Staring in my mirror, I remind myself that I've been through worse. I can handle this. Changing into something more flattering and tighter round my chest, I then do my hair, apply a bit of lippy, and spray a generous amount of perfume from the Armani bottle I stole from Lucy's vast collection of scents.

Taking my time, I arrive to find Greg waiting outside. He smiles and we make small talk before I suggest we head inside to grab a cuppa. He steps ahead of me and opens the door like a true gent before placing his hand on the small of my back. His touch feels nice. When I enter the busy café, the cacophony of chatter comes at me from all sides. A child wails from a buggy near the counter while his mum juggles her purse, phone, and latte, trying to keep a firm grip on the handle to steer herself away. The pungent aroma of freshly brewed coffee hangs fills the air as I take my seat at one table, waiting for Greg, who orders for us both.

As Greg makes his way over to me, I recall that conversation I overheard between him and his friends at the gym when they were bitching about their marriages. That since having children, sex was rare, and their wives were too tired or unwilling to pamper themselves. I remember Greg mentioning Lucy always curling up in bed by nine p.m., leaving him to watch movies or football downstairs on Sky Sports, even though he loathed football. His friends laughed, empathising with his plight.

Now I'll use that memory to my advantage. Greg sits

down across from me. His hazel eyes look weary, hinting at the strain in his marriage.

"Thank you for coming. I hope I'm not speaking out of turn, but I'm worried about Lucy," I confess, wringing my hands like I actually care. "Her behaviour has been so erratic lately, and she's been staring at me, which is unsettling. I know she wants me to leave, and I will, because I'm not sure how much more I can take. I don't want to say anything to her or cause a scene, especially because I know she's under so much stress at the moment."

Greg's expression turns sombre as he stares at his coffee. "I know what you're saying, and I appreciate your concern. It's not about you. Honest. Lucy's struggling at the moment. She's got so much on her plate and sometimes it all gets too much for her." He hesitates, glancing round before lowering his voice. "This morning, Lucy spoke to my mum on the phone, and it was... well, let's say she was short with her. It upsets me she can't seem to handle much stress without lashing out at those closest to her. She's been like this since I first met her. To be honest, I don't know what to do."

I toy with the edge of my coffee cup. "I guess it's not personal, but I feel uneasy round her. I want to be there to support her and the children, but I need to be happy in my job and with her wanting me gone, I really need to know what you both want?"

"I know, Alice. I get it. You don't deserve to feel uncomfortable in our home, and well I'm not sure where this is going to go. I'm sorry if Lucy does finally decides that she doesn't want a nanny. Perhaps it's not for us. But we don't want to upset you."

"Thanks for understanding," I say, my voice laced with a subtle relief that masks my true intentions. I force a sigh and drop my shoulders. "It's not my intention to cause any problems between you and Lucy. Your marriage is important, and I don't want to be the one driving a wedge between you." I look at his face, the deep lines of tension now etched into his features. I can see the exhaustion and frustration in every subtle expression. This is my chance to push him further.

With a warm smile, I reach out and place my hand over his, giving it a reassuring squeeze as I hold his gaze. "Greg, with the right help for her, she's going to be okay."

He blinks in surprise at my touch, as if physical contact has become an alien thing to him. Blushing, he rolls his eyes before sliding his hand away from beneath mine. That's cool for now. I only need to weaken him, and every little gesture chips away at his armour.

"Thanks, Alice," he murmurs, uncomfortable but accepting of my sentiment. "It's difficult trying to keep everything together for the kids when everything is falling apart round me."

"Of course." My mind races. Plotting. Strategizing. Considering how I can push even more while still flying underneath the radar. "But remember, you're not alone. I'm here for everyone."

Greg pauses for a moment, his gaze stopping on a mural on the wall before he looks at me again. "Thank you. How would you feel if you stayed with us for a few days, so Lucy feels more supported? I can suggest it to her when I get home. And if it doesn't work, we can talk to the agency about finding you another position elsewhere?"

I push out a smile, acting surprised at his suggestion. Would being closer to them help me? It's tempting, but it could backfire big time. "I appreciate your offer and I can see why," I say, choosing my words. "But I'm not sure that's a good idea considering Lucy's current mental health and how she feels about me. She's been so hostile towards me.

My being there so much could end up being too much for her."

He leans back in his chair, crossing his arms. "You've been great with the kids. We can take turns looking after them and give Lucy time off until she and I can figure out what's best for her and our family."

My jaw clenches, frustration surging through me. How can he be so blind? I laugh. "Are you sure you're not trying to get in my good books?" I joke, hoping to defuse the situation.

His lips form into a small smile. "That may be part of it," he admits, but then grows serious again. "But, Alice, I think it could make a difference. For all of us. And if it doesn't help or work out then at least we tried."

My jaw tightens as I clench my hands beneath the table to keep them steady. He's persistent, I'll give him that. "Alright, if you think it's for the best."

"Thank you," he says, relief clear in his voice. "I'll talk to Lucy tonight and let you know." Greg pushes his chair back and stands up. "I was worried you'd think I was being stupid."

"Of course not." My tone drips with fake concern. "I'm here to help, remember?" I smirk at the irony of my words.

He nods, rubbing a hand over his face. "You do not know how much I appreciate this. Work has been relentless, and all I want is to come home and spend quality time with Lucy and the kids. But with everything going on... I hide in my study for downtime. It's just too mentally exhausting in the evenings when Lucy seems to be at her worst."

"Believe me, I understand." I lay it on thick, hoping to amplify his sense of isolation. "And I'm glad we had this chat. You shouldn't have to deal with everything alone. That's why I'm here, to ease your burden."

As we make our way out of the café, I take the lead, guiding him by placing a hand on the small of his back this time. He doesn't seem to mind the contact, which sends a thrill down my spine. Outside on the pavement, I pull him into a hug, one that lingers a moment too long. As I hold him close, I can feel his heart beating against his chest, betraying his calm exterior.

"Take care," I whisper into his ear before releasing him from my embrace. Our eyes lock for a second, and I see something flicker within them. A hunger, perhaps?

"Bye, Alice," he murmurs, seemingly dazed from our intimate moment.

I turn away, pushing down a satisfied grin. *Jesus, men are pathetic. And so damn predictable.* With Lucy out of the picture soon enough and after giving Greg time to grieve, I'll be sharing his marital bed. As I walk away, I glance over my shoulder one last time. Greg's still standing there watching me, his expression hard to read. Confusion? For now, though, I have work to do. Destroying Lucy. But the prize at the end, Greg Butler, wrapped round my little finger, which will be worth everything I do now.

29

LUCY

LATER THAT EVENING, after putting the kids to bed, I sit on the sofa nursing a cup of tea I made an hour ago as I wait for Greg to come home. The door opens, and Greg walks in looking tired.

"Lucy, we need to talk. I've been thinking about Alice." He runs a hand through his hair.

My breath is shallow as my body stiffens expecting the worst. My thoughts of confronting him take a hammer blow as I'm thrown off. He's going to tell me he's in love with Alice and wants out of our marriage.

"I think it would be helpful if Alice stayed over a bit more on certain nights. What do you think? She could help a lot more when I'm out with media clients and not back until the early hours."

My jaw clenches, and I can feel my nails digging into the palms of my hands. Waves of rage lap at my insides until I can't hold back any more. I have to say something before I implode. "What were you doing with her at the coffee shop today? I know about you and Alice. I saw you two at the café together with your arm around her. Don't you dare bloody deny it."

Greg stops and stares at me.

"Lucy, you've got it all wrong!" he shouts back, shaking his head. "Alice called me, worried about you. We met up to discuss what's been going on with you. That's all."

"Really, Greg? You expect me to believe that?" I spit. My hands feel restless as I struggle to contain the emotions boiling beneath the surface. "You two are sneaking round behind my back, and now you're trying to convince me to think I'm the one with the bloody problem?"

"Lucy, you need to calm down and think about what you're saying. Nothing is going on between me and Alice. I love you."

"How can I trust you when all you do is lie to me?"

His brow furrows and it's a few seconds before he replies. "Lucy, it was just a friendly catch-up. I didn't think you'd have a problem with it."

My vision blurs with tears, and I struggle to keep them at bay. I stare at Greg, my heart pounding like a pneumatic drill as anger and confusion course through me. "No." My voice trembles with suppressed rage. "Alice is not moving into our home."

"You're overreacting, sweetheart. She's offered to help out when I'm not around. That's all. I had a talk with her and I think having Alice closer at hand would be good and free up more time for you and make everything less stressful. That way we can properly assess her as a person and her possible ongoing role within our family."

"Overreacting?" I hiss, clenching my fists. The image of him touching Alice is imprinted into my mind, and I can't shake it off no matter how hard I try. "I saw you two together today, Greg. You touched her and there were more than friendly smiles. She's young and attractive. Don't tell me you haven't looked at her like *that*. I know what's going on."

"There is no *that*. Nothing is going on. I'm her employer. You're letting your imagination run wild, again."

My breaths come in shallow gasps as I search for words that will make him understand. "I don't want her here, Greg." My voice cracks with raw emotion. "Please, don't do this to us. She's trouble."

"Lucy, I'm trying to help you." His jaw tightens, a hint of strain showing in the set of his shoulders. "Your paranoia and instability are getting worse. Alice wants to be there for you."

"Be there for me?" I repeat. "Or be there for you?"

"Stop it, Lucy." My husband's face hardens. "You're going down the wrong path, and I won't let you drag our family with you."

"Really?" I can't let go. I race into the kitchen, my heart a boiling pot of hurt and anger. The cold tiles beneath my feet seem to seep through my skin, chilling me to the bone. I pull open a drawer with shaking hands, rummaging through its cluttered contents until I find the damning evidence, a single condom.

"Look at this!" I storm back into the lounge, colliding with the door frame before thrusting it towards Greg like a weapon. "I found this in your jeans pocket."

His face pales in shock as he stares at the condom. His eyes flicker between my accusatory gaze and the object clutched in my desperate grip.

"Lucy, I've never seen that before," he says, his voice straining with disbelief. "Why would I need a condom? You're on the pill."

"Then how did it get there, huh?" I demand. "Did it

magically land in your pocket from the condom fairy? Are you sleeping with her too?"

"Lucy, please, listen to me," he pleads, taking a step towards me.

But how can I trust him when I need answers? All my mind carries is doubt and suspicion. "I don't know what to believe."

"Lucy, I swear to you, I've done nothing wrong. I don't know where that condom came from, but I'm not having an affair with anyone." Greg reaches out for my hands.

But I can't continue to believe him. Not anymore. I pull away from his touch, desperation welling up inside me. "How am I supposed to lean on you for support? With every passing day, the distance between us grows. You spend more time with her, or Beth, or at work, than with your own family. And then I find this bundle of joy in your pocket." I wave the condom in front of him, my hand shaking.

My husband doesn't speak, his mouth hanging open in a shocked oval.

I swallow the lump in my throat, feeling defeated and even though I want to scream and shout till I'm out of breath, I know it won't change anything. "She's been invading our lives. Can't you see that?"

"Invading our lives? She's trying to help you, Luce. You wanted a nanny!" He rubs his temples. "And what about your drinking? Do you think it's healthy for the kids to see their mother pissed as a fart, so you can barely stand?"

My cheeks flush with anger and shame. "You have no right to bring that up, and I've not touched a drop in days. My drinking has nothing to do with Alice."

"Doesn't it?" His head tilts as he raises one eyebrow.

"Greg, I'm not blind. I saw you two together at the coffee shop. You touched her, guided her inside. It made me sick." Even though I try to tamp it down, my voice breaks with emotion.

"Lucy, that's enough. Your paranoia is spiralling out of control. You need help, and I can't do it alone." As his jaw clenches, his eyes lock intently on mine, a mix of worry and resolve etched in his expression.

"Help? You want to bring her into our home, let her live with us? That's not help, that's betrayal." Tears roll down my cheeks.

"Betrayal? You're the one who's destroying our family with your constant drinking and accusations. If you don't get your act together and work on improving your mental health, you won't have a family left."

His words are a punch to the gut. The thought of losing my family terrifies me, but so does the idea of Alice living with us. "Please. I love you, Greg. I love our children."

"Then prove it," he says firmly, his gaze unwavering. "I'll scrap the idea of her staying here for a few days. Show me you're willing to change for their sake, and we'll figure it out together. But I will not stand by and watch you destroy our family."

"I've not had a drink in a while now. Isn't that a start?"

He nods but remains silent.

"You still haven't explained this. They were in your black jeans in the wash basket." I hold up the condom packet that I've been gripping tight in my palm.

Greg shrugs. "I honestly don't know where it came from. I swear. The last time I wore those jeans was at the gym. Maybe someone, perhaps one of the boys, put it in there for a joke, because I tossed them in the wash when I returned, along with my kit."

I smile and shake my head in disbelief.

As Greg walks out of the room, leaving me alone with

my thoughts, I'm left to wonder if I can be the wife and mother he needs me to be. The remnants of our argument hang heavy in the air while I attempt to regain my composure. Greg's words echo in my mind, threatening to tear me apart from the inside out. My thoughts race, seeking a way to make him understand, to open his eyes to Alice's true nature.

"Greg," I call out, watching his retreating figure pause in the doorway. "Please, listen to me one more time."

He turns to face me, his expression cold. "Lucy, we've been through this. What more do you want me to say?"

"Look at what she's doing to us. Can't you see it?" My eyes plead for him to believe me. "She's driving a wedge between us, and you're letting her."

"Enough. This isn't about Alice. It's about your refusal to admit that you need help and that everything has become too much for you."

The anger that had subsided bubbles up within me again. "Help? You're blind. Look at how she manipulates you."

"Manipulates me?" he shouts, shaking his head. "You have lost your bloody grip on reality. I don't know how to help you."

"Then let me prove it to you," I beg, desperation seeping into my voice. "Give me the chance to show you what Alice is like. Please, Greg." For a moment, he seems to consider my plea, the stern lines of his face softening. But then he sighs, the disappointment returning to his eyes. "I don't know. Even if we gave the agency a week's notice to let Alice go, you'll still follow on your crusade to uncover the truth, won't you?"

"Please, trust me one last time."

He hesitates and turns away grabbing his car keys and heading out, leaving me broken and alone.

30

LUCY

THE DOORBELL CHIMES AGAIN, jolting me from my thoughts as I try to put one foot in front of the other. "One sec, I'm coming!" I shout, trying to compose myself.

Once I unlock the door, Beth's concerned face greets me. Her eyes are wide with worry. "Are you okay? What's happened?"

My mouth opens, but no words come out as my eyes mist over.

"Lucy?" Beth says again, squeezing my arm.

And it all comes crashing down. A dam breaks within me, and tears spill over, streaming down my cheeks. My body shudders with sobs, each one tearing through me with a force that leaves me breathless.

"Hey, hey," Beth murmurs, pulling me into a tight embrace. I cling to her, my body trembling.

"Everything is falling apart," I say between sobs.

Beth rubs my back, but I can't shake the image of Alice and Greg outside Benji's café or the condom packet in his jeans.

"Let's sit down and talk about this," she says, but as I

head towards the lounge, I wonder if anyone can save me now.

Beth guides me towards the sofas, her soft hand still wrapped round my arm. My legs wobble like jelly as I collapse onto the deep cushions, my body still shaking from the wave of emotions flooding my senses. I bury my face in my hands, praying this is a horrible dream.

"Has something happened to Matthew?"

"No, Matthew's fine."

"Then what is it? You can talk to me, you know that, right?" Beth reaches out to touch my hand, her fingers gentle as she strokes my skin.

I glance up at her, tears blurring my vision, my cheeks pink and blotchy. I want to tell Beth so badly. I want to tell her everything, but I'm afraid of what she'll think of me. What if I'm wrong? What if I'm being paranoid?

"You're scaring me."

I swallow hard, my throat drier than the Sahara Desert, as I force myself to speak the words that make me gag. "I... I think... I think Alice might be having an affair with Greg."

Beth's eyes widen in shock, her hand flying to cover her mouth. "What? No, that can't be right."

"That's what I thought too, but..." My hands tremble as they grip the edge of the cushion. "I saw them, Beth. Outside Benji's café. They looked... close. He even had his hand on her back as they went inside." I pause, still shocked as the memory forces itself into my awareness again as I see the scene play out. I hesitate and then continue. "And then I found a condom packet in Greg's jeans."

Beth's wide eyes search mine for clarification that she heard correctly. "Perhaps they were discussing... And the condom could be..." her voice trails off. She stares at the floor looking both embarrassed and uncertain as the words leave her lips as she struggles to suggest any valid reasons.

"Or she wants him all to herself," I say, punching the cushion. "She's behind everything, creating chaos to drive me mad. To steal my husband and my life."

"Okay, okay." Beth holds up her hands. "Jesus… you really think Greg would do that?"

"Then tell me, Beth, what other explanation is there for Alice and Greg's secret meetings and the condom packet? Huh? Give me one good bloody reason why Greg would have a condom in his pocket if he wasn't planning on using it. It's not for me. I'm on the bloody pill."

"Bastard," she mutters.

All I can manage is nod. I'm all out of words.

She opens her mouth to reply, but stops. She looks as lost and confused as I am, and it's clear that she's realising how ridiculous her attempts at rationalising sound.

"Exactly." A sob breaks loose, my anger giving way to despair. "There isn't one." My body trembles with each heaving breath, my heart shattering like fragile pieces of bone china. I'm so confused and scared.

Beth rubs my back before hurrying to the kitchen to make us both a cuppa. She returns a few minutes later and hands me a cup.

"Drink this. It's sweet, but you need it."

I cradle the cup in both hands and stare at the wall, lost in my thoughts.

"What are you going to do?"

"I don't know, Beth. I'm so confused."

"What did Greg say about the condom?"

I shrug. "He swears he knows nothing about it. They were in his jeans he wore to the gym."

"A prank? Nasheed is a bit of a practical joker, isn't he? But then he wouldn't be that stupid, right?"

"If it is, then it's a sick prank," I reply.

"Greg wouldn't cheat. He loves his family too much."

"I wish I could believe that, but maybe the temptation was too much."

We sit in silence for a few minutes. Neither of us knowing what to say, but I welcome the company regardless.

Beth finally leaves and gives me a hug. "Let's talk tomorrow?" she says as I show her to the door. As it clicks shut behind her, I collapse back onto the sofa, my sobs wracking my body. The silence is suffocating. "Greg... Alice... what have you done?" I say into the emptiness, tears streaming down my cheeks as snot clogs my nose.

31

LUCY

I PACE the lounge chewing my nails. My nerves are in tatters, my mind frayed with an underbelly of anger swirling deep within. I reach for my phone and dial Greg's number. I reach his voicemail, and I leave a message, my voice shaking. "Greg, please come home as soon as you can. I need to talk to you."

Over the next hour, I leave three more messages, further desperation creeping into my voice. As I stomp from room to room, I stop by the front window searching for Greg's arrival, and then the kitchen window, looking for shadowy figures that lurk in the treeline beyond our garden. My paranoia grows with each passing minute as I spin through moments of anxiety, fear, and anger.

"Shit," I mutter, trying Alice's number. Another voicemail again. Images flood my mind of Greg and Alice in bed, wrapped in each other's arms. My stomach lurches as I rush to the toilet. The acidic bile scorches my throat.

"Lucy?" Greg's voice breaks through my haze as he arrives, finding me pacing round the house, staring out of each window, looking for signs of anyone. He hands me a parcel that he found on the doormat outside. "This is for you." He places the box on the kitchen worktop, his concern clear. "You're worrying me."

I don't answer right away, struggling to find the words. Instead, I shake my hands as if they're wringing wet and continue pacing, jabbing a finger in his direction every few seconds. My mind races as thoughts tumble over each other.

"Were you with her?"

"No, Luce. Stop. You need to let this go. I'm not seeing Alice or anyone else. This is crazy."

I glare at him. "No. No. There's more to this. You're all screwing with my mind. I need you to listen to me. Something is happening, and I'm terrified."

"I'm trying to help, but I don't know how to. None of this makes sense. I've not seen you this bad since the miscarriage."

With my hands shaking, I step over to the counter and grip the edge to steady myself. My head is spinning, and my tummy somersaulting. There's no writing on the box, no label, nothing. I open it and blink hard trying to focus before gasping as I find candid photos of me coming and going about town. Panic rises in my chest, and I throw the box at Greg, shouting, "This proves it. Someone is stalking me, Greg. Someone is out there."

He catches the box with a concerned frown and inspects its contents. "Lucy," he says, trying to reassure me, "these aren't photos of you around town. They're family pictures from our trip to Spain when we went to Ronda." His voice grows softer, as if trying to break the news. "These photos were in a box in the loft, and I haven't been up there in months. Have you been up there?"

My confusion reaches a boiling point as I sway and

stare at him. "Please, Greg," I plead, tears streaming down my face. "Believe me, I'm not lying about this. I don't know why I saw those photos as something else, but I swear I did."

His expression softens as he wraps an arm round me. "I believe you," he says into my sweaty, lank hair. "Has Alice been up there?"

I shrug. Could she have been up there and found them? But even as he tries to comfort me, my thoughts continue to race. How could I have seen something that wasn't there? And how can I prove to everyone else, and myself, that my fears are real and not the product of my unravelling sanity?

"Greg, someone's messing with my mind."

"Let's take a second and calm down," he urges, holding me tighter to steady me as he runs a finger along my jawline.

I pull away from him. Sweat beads on my forehead, and I swipe it away with the back of my hand while undoing the top few buttons of my blouse. The heat is suffocating, prickling against my skin like a thousand tiny needles.

"Lucy, this isn't healthy. You're going to have a panic attack. You're getting yourself worked up. Slow down and take a few deep breaths."

"Please listen to me." Desperation claws at my throat. "I need someone on my side."

"I am by your side, alright? I've not going anywhere. I believe you think something is wrong, but we need to figure out what's going on here." His voice is firm as he pulls out his mobile from his back pocket. "The first thing we need to do is get you checked by the doctor to make sure you're alright."

"No." I snatch his mobile away before he can dial. "Not yet."

"Lucy, you're not well," he insists, his eyes filled with worry. "You need help. I nearly lost you after we lost our baby. I'm not going to let you fall apart again. You didn't want the help then either, but it helped, didn't it? My Lucy came back to me, as you got better. You can barely stand and your pupils are dilated, your face is red and you're dripping in sweat."

"Help?" I scream, anger flaring within me as I clutch my damp hair. "What kind of help? To lock me away? To keep me away from my kids? So you can move on with life?"

"Of course not." He reaches out to touch my arm.

"Fine, I'll prove it myself," I mutter. In a flash, I yank open the drawer where we keep important papers and documents, and there it is, Alice's CV.

"What are you doing?" Greg asks, but I ignore him. My fingers tremble as I dial one of Alice's previous employers, a reference listed on her CV. The line rings.

"Hello?" a woman answers, her voice crisp and professional.

"Hi, my name... my name... I'm Lucy Butler." I fight to keep my voice steady. "You're listed as a reference for Alice."

"Uh, yes, that's correct," she replies. "Is there something you need to know?"

"Did she ever behave... oddly? Like strange, or pretend to be nice when she wasn't? I mean, did anything strange happen while, you know, while she was working for you?" I stammer, my desperation seeping through every word as I string sentences together.

"Excuse me?" The woman's confusion is palpable. "I'm not sure what you're getting at."

"Please, I need to know if there was anything... anything off about her," I plead, my vision blurring.

"I don't understand what you're asking. Alice was a great employee. If you have a problem with her, I suggest speaking to her or the agency." And with that, she hangs up.

My heart sinks. I cradle the phone in my hands, tears streaming down my cheeks. Perhaps it's all in my head, this twisted holographic world where paranoia has taken root and bloomed into a terrifying reality.

"Lucy?"

I look at Greg. "I don't want to lose you or our family."

Greg wraps his arms round me, holding me close as I weep against his chest. And in that moment, I wonder if the life I've built is slipping away.

32

LUCY

THE MORNING OFFERS NO RESPITE, as I drag myself to the kitchen, feeling like every limb has a bag of concrete attached to it. My eyes are heavy from the lack of sleep, but the relentless obsession with finding evidence against Alice keeps me going. I pour my third cup of black coffee, letting the bitter aroma fill my nostrils, trying to clear my foggy head.

"Lucy," Greg's voice comes through the door. "You look like crap. You should call in sick today."

"I already have. They weren't happy, but I told them I was up most of the night with a tummy bug so would work from home today and get on with the sample reviews." Taking a sip of my coffee, I wince at the burning sensation that scorches my throat. But at least it's helping to keep me awake.

The kids are still asleep, and I have time to work on my ideas before they need me. Despite Greg's admonishments, I've spent most of the night digging into Alice's past, trying to find anything, even the slightest sliver of information that might expose her for who she is. So far, all I've found are dead ends, and my mind feels like it's giving up the will to live.

I stare at my laptop screen and my debit card that sits beside me on the kitchen counter. Greg's not around, so with a quick click, I pay for premium access to background checks. If there's something hidden in Alice's past, I *will* find it.

"Is this what you've become?" I whisper, my voice tired with exhaustion and desperation. I tap my fingers on the counter as I wait for the results. "Come on, come on."

My eyes dart back and forth between the screen of my laptop and the doorway, like I'm expecting Greg to reappear and catch me.

"Gotcha!" I exclaim when the results load, my eyes wide and glued to the information. I lean in closer, almost pressing my nose to the screen as I scan the data. But instead of the breakthrough I hoped for, I'm met with more frustration.

"Shit." I sigh, slamming my hand on the counter and making my coffee cup jump. The search results are incomplete, leaving me no closer to discovering the truth about Alice. But I can't give up now; I won't let her win.

"Lucy, what's going on?" Greg appears in the doorway, his face creased with worry. I don't have time for this. He doesn't understand the urgency of my quest.

"Nothing. Just doing some work." I turn my attention back to my laptop. I lean in closer to my screen, scrolling through pages of information, willing something to reveal itself. I've so many pages open, it's hard to flick between them all. And then there it is. My pulse quickens as my eyes settle on the discovery. No records of Alice exist before the age of eighteen. No schools, no birth certificate. Nothing.

"Greg!" I shout, unable to contain my excitement.

"Look at this. I've found something. There's nothing about her before she turned eighteen. That's not normal. No one just magically appears at eighteen. Please take a look."

"Alright." Greg joins me in the kitchen and peers over my shoulder at the screen. He glances over the information and narrows his eyes. "That seems strange. But it could be a mistake."

"A mistake? This isn't a mistake," I exclaim, feeling vindicated. "She's hiding something, I know it. And I won't stop until I find out what."

Greg places a hand on my shoulder. "Is it worth it? If she bothers you that much, we'll get rid of her."

"Of course it is," I cry out, pushing his hand away. "Don't you see? She's manipulating us. You, me, Beth, everyone. I do want her gone but I also need to find out the truth."

He sighs. "I'm not sure what to say any more, Luce. I love you, but this crazy fixation is changing you. Every day, more and more of the woman I love is slipping away." Greg's voice cracks as his gaze locks with mine. "I thought today might be different when you promised to let this go, but I can see that's not happening. I've had enough. Let me talk to the agency and arrange for her to leave, and in return, you drop this quest to search for the truth?"

"Greg, I …" My voice falters as I search for the words, my hands trembling on his arm.

"Lucy," he says gently, prising my fingers off him, "you need help. You're tearing yourself apart over this and damaging us. Who cares about her past? She's upsetting you enough for us to let her go and draw a line under it and move on."

Hurt by his rejection, I snatch my hand back. "Someone erased her past. This is exactly what I expected to find."

"Lucy—" he begins, but I don't give him the chance to finish.

"Fine. If you won't listen, then I'll find someone who will."

"Lucy…" Greg starts, but I spin round to face him, my anger boiling over.

"Don't you dare say anything!" I bare my teeth in anger.

"I can't do this anymore," he whispers, his voice breaking.

"No, Greg, it's not me." I clutch the sides of my head. "It's her. Can't you see what she's doing to us? To our family?"

"Enough." He pulls away and paces round the hallway. "I won't let you drag us all down this rabbit hole any further. You need help, real help, and until you get it, I can't support you in this. My priority has to be the well-being of the kids and your safety."

"Greg, please." The words escape me, barely a whisper, but he turns away.

Desperation claws at me, a silent scream in the void he leaves. I feel so empty inside. So alone. My heart throbs, each strangled beat echoing the finality of my resolve. It's rising from the ashes of betrayal and spurred on by a burning need for the truth. If no one else will stand by me to peel away Alice's web of deceit, then I'll tread that path myself.

Whatever it takes.

33

ALICE

DAY BY DAY, I watch Lucy's pathetic world crumble round her like a sandcastle being washed away by the incoming tide. My plan is working better than I ever dared to imagine. The zopiclone has been doing its job, and she frequently stares into space, her lips muttering silent words. It's almost comical, and I have to clench my jaw to fight the urge to laugh. Perhaps they're silent prayers.

I remember one particular day when Lucy was walking round in a near-catatonic state on the landing. "Lucy, are you feeling alright?" I asked. She jumped a little at the sound of my voice, lost in her bewildered state.

"Y-yeah, tired, that's all," she stuttered, her eyes wide with confusion. I could tell she was trying to piece together her thoughts, but it was like watching someone trying to catch water in their fingers. Her once-animated gestures were slow and uncertain.

"I think you should lie down for a while," I suggested, my heart pounding as the voice inside my head kept chanting, "Do it. Do it. Do it." As I glanced down the stairs, I pictured her body rolling head over heels and lying motionless in a crumpled heap.

As I helped her to her bedroom, my mood switched from dark amusement to seething hatred. There are fleeting moments when I want to shove her down the stairs. There have been a few occasions where the opportunity presented itself over recent weeks. Then sometimes I hate her so much that I want to run a knife across her belly and watch as her innards spill out over the floor. But that would be too quick a death for her.

As I now stare at my reflection in my rear-view mirror, I want Lucy to be so broken that she spends the rest of her life in a psychiatric hospital, cut off from her friends, husband, and kids. I want her drugged up to her eyeballs, so she doesn't even know what day it is.

That would be perfect. Without Lucy in the equation, Greg will need a full-time nanny to care for his kids while he works. Who better to take up the role than me? He'd be dependent on me, and the kids already love me enough for him to trust me to look after them.

I ponder on how Greg would grieve for the marriage and family life he once had. Time is a great healer, so they say, and well, men have needs. I know it won't be long before Greg gets so lonely that he turns to me for comfort and support. The thought sends a shiver down my spine, as excitement rushes through me.

"Greg," I say to my reflection, imagining his arms wrapped round me, his lips pressed against mine. "You'll see how much better I am for you than Lucy ever was." I give it six months before he's shagging me.

The hum of the car engine vibrates through me as I grip the steering wheel and pull away from the kerb. "Almost there," I say to myself, navigating through the quiet, leafy streets of their quaint neighbourhood. Each turn brings me closer to her, closer to her life I've been so desperate to destroy.

As I head to Lucy's, I picture Greg's face when he realises how perfect we are together. I imagine him breaking down in my arms, his tears staining my skin as I provide the comfort he's been seeking. "Stupid cow," I hiss under my breath, feeling the anger bubble up inside me again as I think of Lucy. How dare she take him for granted? How dare she carry on with life?

As I drive, I replay the moments leading up to this point. Each minor victory, each step that brought me closer to my goal. And now, as I head towards the Butlers' home once more, I can almost see the end. "Enjoy your last days, Lucy." A twisted grin spreads across my face. "Because soon, everything you hold so dear to you will be gone."

My eyes widen in surprise as I approach the Butlers' drive, my pulse racing with a dangerous mix of excitement and fear. As I step out of the car and head towards the house, I think about what's going to happen next when I see her standing there waiting for me.

34

LUCY

WITH THE KIDS still in bed, I pace up and down the driveway, my heart pounding like a drum in a marching band. The leaves crunch underfoot as I glance at the time on my phone for the umpteenth time. Greg has left for work, and Alice will arrive soon.

"Come on, hurry," I say.

The distant hum of an engine catches my attention, and I see Alice's car turning into our street. My pulse quickens further, and my mouth runs dry. I glimpse her face behind the wheel, her eyes wide with surprise as she sees me waiting for her. As soon as she parks, I march towards her, my finger already accusing her of something before a word has left my lips.

"Who are you?" I shout, my voice shaking with anger and fear. "You've been lying to us, pretending to be someone you're not."

Alice steps from the car, her hands raised. "What do you mean?"

"Don't play the bloody innocent with me! You're hiding something, and I'm going to find out what!" I shout. My mind races with all the things I've noticed. The little slips in her story that makes little sense.

"Please, calm down, Lucy," she shrinks under the pressure of my accusations. "I promise you; I'm not hiding anything. I don't know where you would get such an idea."

My eyes narrow as I watch her. "No, I won't bloody calm down. Is this a sick game to you?" I spit, my voice strained. "Do you enjoy playing with people's lives? Manipulating them like puppets on strings?"

"Lucy, please." Alice's hair falls over her face as she shakes her head. "I would do nothing to hurt you or your family. I want to help. That's what you pay me for."

"Stop lying!" I scream, my emotions boiling over. "I won't let you destroy our lives or me. I'm not a crazy woman who's lost her mind. If you've got nothing to hide, then prove it. Let me search your car."

Alice's brown eyes widen in shock, but she doesn't say no. Instead, she hesitates for a moment and gives a resigned sigh and shrug. "Alright, Lucy. If it makes you feel better, go ahead. Search my car."

I storm over to her car, pull the door open, and begin searching. What I'm searching for, I don't know, but there has to be something to prove I'm right. I look in the glove box, side door bins, even under the front seats. I'm determined to find something, anything, to confirm my suspicions and to prove I'm not going mad.

"Lucy," Alice says from behind me. "Please, be careful. You don't need to tear everything apart."

"Stay back," I warn her, my voice tense and angry. "And let me do this."

But as I continue searching, my heart sinks as I find nothing incriminating. No secret documents or mysterious objects, only the usual clutter of someone's everyday life.

"See?" Alice's voice fills with concern as she stands a safe distance away with her arms folded across her chest. "There's nothing there, Lucy. You're stressed, that's all. It's been a tough time for you."

I slam the car door shut and stare at the empty driveway, my mind a whirlwind of emotions as confusion clouds my thinking. Why is there nothing here? What was I looking for? Is Alice right?

I look at my nanny, who stands there quietly, a mix of sadness and worry etched across her face as she purses her lips. I sigh heavily and run a hand through my hair. Neighbours are peering through their windows curious about the argument and raised voices. I stumble back into the house as I feel the heat of embarrassment creep up my neck. Alice follows me inside, remaining silent.

"Right," she says softly, placing her bag by the stairs. "I'll... I'll wake the kids and get them ready for breakfast." She avoids my gaze, trying to sidestep the awkwardness that now fills the hallway like a dense fog.

"Fine," I mutter, not knowing what else to say. I watch as she disappears towards Matthew's bedroom, the soft thud of her footsteps on the carpet fading away. As soon as I'm sure she's busy, my desire to know the truth gets the better of me. Her purse. There must be something in there, a clue about who she is. I snatch it from inside her handbag on the floor and rummage through its contents, my fingers shaking with fear. Lipstick, tissues, keys... nothing out of the ordinary. But then, tucked away in a compartment, I find it: a business card for Dr Scott, Psychotherapist. My eyes narrow. This could be something or nothing at all, but either way, I need to follow this lead.

I take out my phone and snap a photo of the card before replacing it in Alice's purse. If she's hiding anything, I promise myself I will uncover it as I return her purse to her bag.

"Lucy?" Alice's voice startles me, and I jump. She stands at the top of the stairs, her eyes filled with a strange mixture of concern and confusion. "Is everything okay?"

"Who are you?" I demand again as I back away from the stairs.

Alice hesitates for a moment before taking the stairs down to me, her eyes not leaving me. "Lucy, please," she begs. "I'm Alice. I'm not hiding anything."

"Explain the inconsistencies then," I blurt out, my shaking hands betraying my agitation. "You don't have a past. Your identity is sketchy."

"I don't understand why you think I'm lying." Alice's voice is steady, but her gaze is fixed on the bag on the floor as if knowing what I've been up to. "I... I understand your concerns. But I promise you, I'm not hiding anything bad. I've been nothing but honest with you and your family."

"Oh, really?" I challenge. "Then explain the inconsistencies in your background. Why can't I find anything about your past as a child?"

Alice hesitates, her eyes darting round the hallway as if searching for an escape. She settles her gaze on me, her expression one of vulnerability and heartache. "Lucy, I... I had a tough childhood." The words tumble out, almost reluctantly. "I've spent years trying to put it behind me. I changed my name as a fresh start. That's why pieces might be missing. But I assure you, I've been honest about everything else."

"Maybe you have." My voice wavers between anger and sympathy. "But I refuse to believe that's the whole truth."

Alice grabs her handbag and clutches it to her chest. "I'm not your enemy. Can't you see that?" Her words leave me feeling like I'm wading through a fog of uncertainty. They paint a picture of hardship, but the brushstrokes feel too calculated, too rehearsed.

My eyes narrow slightly, my voice steady despite the storm of emotions inside. "There's something you're not telling us." It's more than a statement—it's a conviction, a knowing that behind Alice's mask of vulnerability lies a truth yet to be unravelled.

Alice chokes back a sob, her eyes moist with tears. She gives me one last pleading look before sidestepping me and storming out of the front door, her footsteps echoing through the hallway.

As I watch her run down the drive, a touch of guilt spread inside me. What have I done? I stand there in the empty hallway, the silence deafening, my fingertips grazing the cold surface of my phone as I pull it from my pocket.

A screenshot.

One emblazoned with the name of Dr Scott, Psychotherapist. A simple business card, frozen in digital form. More than that, a clue, a key, a window into the enigma that is Alice and the lead I need.

35

LUCY

THE PHONE in my hand reminds me of what I need to do next, though I'm not sure I want to face it. But I can't wait any longer as desperation gnaws away at me like a hungry rat. I don't know if I'm making progress, but I have very few options left. How many more times will I have to look at Alice's smug face without knowing the truth? I'm not even sure she'll return after what happened.

I tut as I press at my screen, realising that I have to call Dr Scott's number after finding it inside Alice's purse. It feels like forever as the line rings, and when someone answers, I gasp in surprise.

"Dr Scott speaking," he answers in a professional tone.

"Erm... um... Dr Scott, my name is Mrs Lucy Butler." I pause, unsure how to continue as embarrassment flushes my face. "I found your card in our nanny's purse, Alice Simpson. I was wondering if you could tell me why she might have it."

"Mrs Butler, I'm afraid I cannot discuss my work or clients with anyone unless it's with another professional colleague, the police, or a mental health unit," he says, his voice guarded and cautious.

"Please, Dr Scott. Things are going wrong for me and my family, and I believe Alice may have a part to play in it. Someone has been stalking me, my car has been vandalised, and things are being moved around my house. I know it sounds crazy, but our lives are falling apart, my mental health has taken a hit, and I need help to understand what's going on."

For a moment, there's silence on the line. Then Dr Scott's tone shifts, softening with concern. "I understand that you're worried, Mrs Butler. I can't discuss each individual case, but I'll check my old case files and see if there's any reference to this individual. If I find anything, I'll get back to you."

"Thank you," I breathe. Relief floods over me like a torrent. After he gets my details, I hang up the phone, my hands shaking with a mix of anticipation and dread. What will Dr Scott's search reveal? And how will those revelations change everything I thought I knew about Alice?

With each passing minute, my thoughts spiral further into darkness. I pace round the house. After the kids have breakfast, I settle them in Matthew's room with a DVD. Every few minutes I peek through the windows looking for Alice. I rush to my bedroom to check if anyone is watching us from the treeline beyond our garden, and then ensure that I've locked all the windows and doors. My fingers tap on the kitchen counter as I watch the screen on my phone, willing it to come to life with an incoming call. My mind works overtime, coming up with a litany of terrible things that could lurk in Alice's past like sinister motives, hidden traumas, or worse.

After an agonising hour, my phone buzzes. It's Dr

Scott. I snatch it up at once. "Hello?" The word leaps from my mouth.

"Mrs Butler, it's Dr Scott. I understand your concern, but I'm afraid I cannot disclose any specific information because of patient confidentiality. If there's something concerning you, I suggest you call the police." His tone apologetic, yet firm.

"Dr Scott, I need to know if I should be worried about anything."

"Mrs Butler, I'm sorry, but my professional ethics prevent me from revealing anything further," he insists.

My fists clench in frustration, my nails digging into my palms. If Dr Scott won't help me, then I'll have to uncover Alice's secrets myself. But how? The silence on the other end of the line feels final as Dr Scott won't budge, but I have to try.

"Dr Scott, please," I plead. "If you can't tell me anything about Alice, could you at least speak with her? I'm worried."

"I'm sorry. Please contact the police if you have any serious concerns," he says, the reluctance clear in his voice.

"Thank you for your time," I say with a sigh, before hanging up.

As I lower the phone and place it on the worktop, an image of Alice flashes in my mind, her delicate features, the way her brown eyes seem to hold secrets far too deep for someone her age. What could be lurking beneath that calm exterior?

I sit in the lounge hugging a cushion, hoping to dampen my growing anxiety. I replay every moment with Alice, scrutinising every one of her words and gestures for a hidden meaning, but there are too many crowding my mind, which only makes me feel worse. Willing myself to focus, I sway back and forth, trying to control the chaos that is my life.

I finally get up, impatience getting to me as I once again check all the windows and doors even though no one has come or gone.

36

ALICE

The salty taste of my crocodile tears lingers on my lips as I wipe them away. A smirk curls the corners of my mouth as I take a glance at myself in the vanity mirror above my steering wheel. When I told Greg about Lucy's crazy outburst, he stuttered with shock and sadness.

"Sorry I couldn't stay, Greg," I told him, my voice quivering with feigned distress.

His concern for me was genuine, and his words carried a softness that felt like a warm, cosy duvet wrapped round me. Mission accomplished.

With a heavy sigh, I step from the car and make my way back into my apartment. The familiar creak of the floorboards follows me as I head towards the spare bedroom, the sanctuary where I can still feel connected with Jordan. The wall of clippings, photos, and cryptic notes smothers me. It's both comforting and upsetting as my eyes dart from one article to another. My phone shatters the silence as it vibrates in my back pocket, startling me. My brow furrows as an unfamiliar number flashes on the screen. I answer it.

"Hello?"

"Ah, Alice, it's Dr Scott," comes the voice from the other end, one I haven't heard in years. A chill runs down my spine, nerves prickling my skin that sends an unease through me. What could he want after all this time?

"Dr Scott? I... How did you get this number?" I try to keep the unease from seeping into my tone.

"Never mind that." He brushes off my question in his customary placid manner. "It's been a few years since we last spoke. I've been thinking about you and thought I should check in."

His voice is gentle, but listening to him and his tone threatens to unravel me. Why now? What does he know? My grip on the phone tightens as I slide down against the wall, its cold surface sending a shiver through me as I pull my knees up to my chest.

"Thank you, Dr Scott," I say. "But it's unnecessary. I'm doing fine now."

"Are you?" Dr Scott questions, his tone layered with concern and a hint of scepticism that I am all too familiar with. "You have attended none of your follow-up appointments since our last meeting three years ago."

Surprised by his persistence, I struggle to think of what to say. I need him off my back and I need to convince him enough to not escalate this up the chain. Looking round the spare bedroom, my gaze falls on the wall of clippings again. The familiar anxiety spreads through me. The same bodily sensations that I felt so often while in his consulting room staring at the ceiling as I bared my soul to him. But I was better than him. I never told him *everything* about that day when I lost Jordan.

"Dr Scott," I begin, taking a deep breath, attempting to steady my quivering voice. "I appreciate your concern, but my past is just that—the past, and I have you to thank for that. You helped me to move forward. I'm in a much better place now." I try to sound as confident and self-assured as possible, but my chest tightens.

"That's good to hear. Moving on can be a healthy thing, Alice." But he doesn't sound convinced. "But ignoring deeply buried unresolved issues can also lead to future problems. Mental health isn't something we can take lightly. When the police couldn't find the hit-and-run driver who killed your brother, I know that was difficult for you to accept."

His words rattle through my mind, threatening to resurface all those memories I've fought so intensely to bury. I swallow hard, trying to push back the wave of emotions. His voice always had a knack for doing that. Perhaps it was his training, or our connection. I don't know, but it always scared me to feel so vulnerable in his presence.

"Dr Scott," my voice breaks despite my best efforts to stay composed, "I'm doing well. I don't need further appointments or therapy. It *was* voluntary, after all. I've coped and moved forward." I grip my phone, knuckles whitening as I fight to keep my composure. Despite Dr Scott's gentle but probing tone, I feel cornered.

"I understand that you're nannying for a new family now. The Butlers. Is that wise?"

My heart stutters. How does he know? The walls of my carefully constructed reality seem to crumble round me. "How did you find out about that?" I demand.

Dr Scott doesn't answer my question. Instead, he pushes on, his tone unwavering. "Please, Alice, I need to understand."

My stomach clenches as I force myself to swallow. "I've forgiven and moved on. I see this job as part of my healing process. Lucy and Greg have been good to me, and the children are fantastic," I begin. "Jordan's death was… unfortunate, but it was an accident. No one could have foreseen what happened."

"Perhaps," Dr Scott concedes. "But I believe there might be more to it than that. Sometimes, our past has a way of resurfacing when we least expect it to, and it affects those around us."

"Seriously, I'm doing well now. There's no need to worry."

"How have you been processing your own emotions about Jordan's death?"

I grow quiet, my throat tightening as I fight to find words. The past lingers like a dark cloud over me, refusing to go away. "I've made peace with what happened," I lie. "I don't want to dwell on it."

"Repression is not the same as making peace," he counters. "You've hidden away your pain, but it's still there, waiting to resurface. When you do that, it often never goes away completely."

"Please, leave me alone," I plead, my voice cracking.

"Confronting your repressed emotions can be painful, yes," Dr Scott says, "but it's the only way to move forward."

"I know."

"Look, it's normal to have repressed these memories. Our young minds often protect us from the most painful events in our lives by burying them deep within our subconscious, so that we can carry on with life."

"So, you're saying that there's more to my past with Jordan that I don't remember?"

"Exactly. Repressed memory syndrome is a common way for our brains to cope with traumatic experiences. And while it may have protected you for a time, now it's crucial for your healing to bring those memories to light."

Despite his soothing voice, the thought of uncovering

The Perfect Nanny

more hidden pain terrifies me. A shiver runs down my spine and my hands tremble.

"Would you consider meeting with me in person again? I think it would be beneficial. We could work together to explore these memories safely. It might be the key to putting this all behind you."

A lump forms in my throat, choking on any response I might have given. Instead, I nod, even though he can't see me through the phone. But then a sudden wave of fear washes over me. No. This is too much.

"Thank you, but I can't... I won't." With that, I end the call, cutting off any chance of him persuading me further.

The silence that follows seems to press in on me from all sides, suffocating me with its weight. What if he's right? What if there's something buried deep within me I've kept hidden for years?

My legs carry me across the room, back to the wall of clippings and photographs. They seem to bore into me. I pace back and forth, my mind a whirlwind of thoughts and emotions, each more distressing than the last.

"Stop it," I say to myself, gripping the sides of my head as if trying to hold everything together, but the voices keep coming. Keep taunting me. "You're fine. Everything is fine. Ignore them."

But the nagging doubt remains festering in my mind. If I let these memories resurface, what kind of person might they reveal me to be? And could I bear to face that truth, whatever it may be?

For now, I pace and hope the answer never comes. "Everything is fine," I say again, but I can't shake the feeling that Dr Scott has unlocked something dark within me, something that I've fought so hard to suppress all these years. My hands clench into fists as I stare at a picture of Jordan.

"Stop it," Jordan says as I close my eyes tight to shut out the thoughts. "You're stronger than this."

"Okay, Jordan," I say aloud. "Think. If your memories resurface... what then?" Would these memories change who I am? Would they reveal a terrible secret that I've hidden even from myself? And if they did, what could I do about it? I hold my arms up to my sides. "Okay. Let's say the worst happens. Let's say there's a dark truth buried within me. What then, Jordan?"

"You confront it. You face whatever it is head-on," he replies, with steely determination in every word.

"Right." I straighten my spine and steel myself for what lies ahead. "Let's do this."

And with that, I turn away from the wall and leave the spare room. There's no turning back now.

37

LUCY

THE FRONT DOOR OPENS, and I hear the heavy thud of Greg's briefcase hitting the floor and his keys rattling as they land on the table in the hallway. His footsteps are weary as he shuffles into the lounge, looking more broken than I've ever seen him.

"Lucy," he rubs his face with his hands as his eyes move to the wine glass in my hand, "what's going on? You said you'd stopped drinking."

I swallow hard, struggling to keep my emotions in check. "I... I've been in contact with Dr Scott, Alice's therapist."

"Therapist? I didn't know she had a therapist. How did you even get those details?" Greg's jaw clenches, his eyes narrowing.

"From her purse," I admit, wincing at how it sounds. I brace myself for his reaction.

"Her bloody purse?" Greg erupts, his face reddening as he undoes the top button on his shirt. "What the hell, Lucy. What are you playing at?"

My head spins, and I fight back the urge to shout back. "I had to know, Greg. Something's not right. I can feel it."

"You went through someone else's belongings? Are you mad? That's not like you, Luce. You've lost the bloody plot. I thought we were going to drop this?"

"No, that's what *you* said we were going to do," I plead, my voice slurred and trembling. "But you're not listening to me. Something is going on. Nothing makes sense anymore." As I stagger towards him, my arms outstretched, the room seems to tilt round me as my vision blurs.

As Greg steps back, a mix of anger and concern fills his eyes. "This has gone too far, Lucy."

He pulls out his phone, and I realise he's about to call for help. Panic surges through me. "No, Greg, please. You don't understand." But my words fall on deaf ears as he calls our doctor. My world feels like it's crumbling round me, and I know I need to prove myself to him. I need to show him I'm not losing it, and that whatever is happening is tearing us apart. But how can I make him see?

Desperation drives me forward as I lunge towards Greg, my fingers outstretched and grasping for the phone. "No!" I scream. He sees me coming and pushes me away. The force of his shove sends me reeling backwards, and I tumble onto the sofa. My wine glass slips from my hand, shattering on the floor and spraying crimson droplets across the once-pristine cream carpet.

"Lucy." Greg's voice is a mixture of anger and disbelief. But he doesn't have time to deal with the mess; he's too busy redialling on his phone. "Beth," he mutters under his breath, desperation creeping into his tone.

I try to speak but nothing comes out as I try to regain my balance and focus while the room revolves around me.

My mind fights to find clarity amid the avalanche of emotions. "Please don't do this..." Greg seems unfazed by my plea. He fixes his attention on the phone, frustration etched into the lines of his face when Beth doesn't answer.

"Shit," he curses, before cutting off the call. For a moment, hope rises within me. Maybe he'll reconsider and listen to me. But I'm so wrong.

"I can't watch you destroy yourself like this." His words cut into me, each syllable like a shard of glass tearing at my skin.

"Greg... I... We... Figure it out. Pleeease, let's talk about it," I slur as I struggle to my feet. My legs wobble beneath me as I fight to regain control of my body. But everything I say does little to change Greg's manner.

Greg throws his hands up in surrender. "That's it. I can't do this anymore. You're coming with me and we're dropping the kids at my Mum's. Then I'm taking you to the hospital. Mum will be fine with the short notice and understand the urgency. I'm worried about you and we can't go on like this."

As he turns to gather the kids and their belongings, my vision blurs with tears. A part of me wants to cling to him and tell him we can work this out, but another part insists that he's betrayed me and not stood by me.

I lunge forward to grab his arm. "Don't, Greg."

"Enough, Luce." My husband's eyes darken with frustration. He strides towards me, and before I can react, his hands are on my shoulders, pushing me back onto the sofa and then taking a seat beside me. He takes my hands in his and holds them tight. "Lucy, we're going to the hospital. Final. I just want to make sure you're okay. You're not yourself. I get it you're upset, and you think Alice is bad news. If she is, then we need proof she's behind this. That way we can tell the agency and they can ensure she can't cause trouble for any other family."

Greg sighs as his shoulders drop. "I know how all these things with the damage to the car, the pictures, what you've seen outside, and the jewellery being moved have affected you. I agree, and on the face of it, it's all happened since Alice's arrival. But unless we have proof, we can't go to the police or the agency."

I feel a sense of relief knowing that Greg is actually listening and is on my side for a change.

"But first, let's get you properly checked out, hey?"

I give in even though I don't want to go.

38

ALICE

The evening is heavy with the scent of rain, and it hangs in the air as I sit alone in my lounge. Dr Scott's words still echo in my mind, but it's Jordan's voice that drowns everything else out. He was always right; growing up, he never hesitated to remind me of that fact.

I sink into the worn sofa, feeling its familiar embrace as I reach for a small leather case on the floor. Its contents are so precious to me: my mum's old diary, filled with private thoughts. My fingers trace the embossed pattern of the worn leather cover before opening it, revealing the entries describing the accident that changed everything.

June 17th,

Jordan's condition hasn't improved. The doctors say that the swelling in his brain isn't going down, and they don't know if he'll ever wake up. His body is broken, bones snapped like little twigs. I can't breathe when I look at him. I would do anything to swap places with him. All those times he was naughty, all the harsh words we exchanged... And now, he might never speak to me again.

My heart aches as I read the words scrawled in Mum's handwriting. The memory of Jordan's unresponsive form in the hospital bed fills my vision, threatening to drown me in sorrow. But I force myself to continue.

June 29th,

Today marks two weeks since the accident. People keep telling me it wasn't her fault, but I can see the doubt in their eyes. I know they wonder why she was there, why she didn't save him. Sometimes, late at night when I'm lying in bed, I wonder the same thing.

July 10th,

We visited Jordan today. We stood there holding each other and crying softly. There's no sign of improvement and as each day passes, the doctor seems less optimistic. Please wake up.

Tears blur the ink on the page as I read, and I feel a tight knot forming in the pit of my stomach. For years, I have suppressed these memories, hidden behind the façade of a quiet, well-adjusted young woman. But now, with Dr Scott dragging me back into involuntary therapy, and Jordan's voice haunting me, I know the truth is coming.

August 2nd,

They have declared Jordan brain-dead. They are going to turn off his life support tomorrow. I can't bear it. My son, my baby boy. The light in our life will be gone forever. And it's all because of her.

THE FINALITY of that last entry hangs in the air like a heavy shroud, suffocating me with its weight. As much as I want to deny it, I know deep down that Jordan was right and I need to make things right.

MY HEAD POUNDS as flickers of deeper memories try to break through. The pressure in my brain threatens to crack my skull, so I scratch at my arms with my long nails. The raised grazes and redness are a painful distraction for me. I focus on the stinging sensation, trying to keep the threatening memories at bay.

DESPITE MY DESPERATE attempts to tamp them down, the memories consume me. Glimpses of Jordan's laughter, his teasing smile, and the warmth of our shared childhood moments flash before my eyes like an old grainy movie. My heart aches, and I know I can't escape what is coming. I fight the memories as they gain further traction, and I'm terrified of what lies in the recesses of my mind. I bite my lip, drawing blood, and try to force my thoughts elsewhere, to the smell of coffee in Benji's café as I sit across the table with Greg, to the giggly naughtiness of Sarah as I chase her round the garden, to anything that isn't my distant past. But as much as I attempt to control them, the dark memories refuse to be contained any longer.

. . .

"Stop it," I cry out, my voice cracking as the memories surge forward like a tidal wave.

I feel myself crumbling, and brace myself for the impact. The truth will come, whether or not I am ready. And I can only hope that when it does, I will have the strength to face it and make things right, for Jordan, for myself, and for everyone caught up in our tragedy. As the memories continue to flood my consciousness, I grit my teeth, digging my nails deeper into my arm, determined to survive the onslaught as the screaming inside my mind gets louder.

The memories blur but grow clearer with each agonising moment. I toss my head back and clamp my eyes shut. Jordan's laugh echoes through my mind as he teases me, his voice once warm and familiar, now unsettling in its persistence. I can feel my anger rising, as if it were happening right now.

"Leave me alone!" I shout at him, my heart pounding in my chest. But Jordan just smirks. The argument becomes more intense.

"Come on, Alice," he taunts, taking off down the street. "What are you waiting for? Catch me if you can."

. . .

My legs move as if they have a mind of their own, chasing after him despite the part of me that screams at me not to. "Jordan," I call out. "Please stop." But he doesn't listen, and I am powerless to make him.

The diary slips from my hands, falling to the floor with a soft thud. My pulse races, fear, and adrenaline coursing through me like an out-of-control tornado. I rise to my feet, half-blind with panic, and race to my bed.

"Make it stop," I beg, clutching the sides of my head. "Please, make it stop." The noise is deafening, a cacophony of ghoulish voices and emotions that are tearing me apart from the inside. I'm scared of what I've unleashed upon myself. "Jordan." Tears stream down my face as I catch my breath. "I didn't mean it. I never meant for any of this to happen."

But the memories are relentless, forcing me to confront the darkness that has festered within me for far too long. My body writhes and trembles beneath the weight of it all, the pain and guilt overwhelming me with a ferocity I've never experienced before.

The room spins round me. Jordan's voice echoes in my mind, his laughter taunting me as he dares me to catch up. "Come on, Alice, what are you waiting for?" he sneers.

. . .

"Jordan, I swear..." My words dissolve into a choked sob, the force of my anguish threatening to suffocate me as the memories keep pelting me like machine-gun fire. "I hope you die!" I scream at him, only to watch in horror as he runs into the street and is hit by a passing car. The sickening thud as the car connects with Jordan's body. Then everything goes silent. It's as if the world has come to a standstill. "Get away from me!" I scream as a woman's arm wraps round me, attempting to offer comfort. But her touch feels constricting while I battle to wriggle free.

"No," I whimper, tossing and turning in bed, unable to find a reprieve from the gnawing guilt that claws at me. Frustration surfaces, and I punch my pillows, trying to release the pent-up emotions that threaten to consume me.

"Please. I just want Jordan back," I beg, burying my head in the pillows, my throat raw and sore from screaming.

"Jordan." Frantic, I clutch at my hair. "It wasn't me driving. It was her. What have I done? Please forgive me. I'm sorry." Tears blur my vision as I look to the ceiling, seeking answers in the darkness that surrounds me.

That scene keeps looping back to the beginning, forcing me to relive the horror.

. . .

The Perfect Nanny

"Sorry won't change anything," comes the cruel reply. Jordan's here. I can sense him. "You did this, Alice."

"No, it was an accident," I protest.

"An accident you could have prevented." The words sting like a slap, bringing fresh tears to my eyes. "You wished me dead, Alice. And now, here we are."

"Please, don't say that. I never planned for any of this." I sob, feeling my guilt bear down upon me like a crushing vice.

"Doesn't matter now, does it?" The relentless assault continues. "I'm gone, Alice. Because of you."

"Enough. I can't take it anymore." I gasp, the pain becoming too much to bear.

"Then let me help you. Together, we can face anything," his voice urges, warm and inviting.

With a heavy sigh, I drag myself up from my bed, my legs trembling. The first light of dawn filters through the curtains. "Alright, Jordan. I'll do this for you, and for myself. I'll get revenge for you, no matter how painful it may be."

39

LUCY

THE MORNING LIGHT pierces through a gap in the curtains, its rays hitting my throbbing head as I drag myself off the bed. My body feels exhausted, and my mind is an utter mess. Rubbing my sore eyes, I stare out the window at the woods beyond, recollecting morsels of memories of last night's events.

I remember feeling so broken as I sat and watched the kids go into Greg's mums before we drove to the hospital. How did it come to this?. We sat in A & E for an eternity, surrounded by the moans and groans of other patients. After four long hours and a blood test, a doctor assessed me and referred me to the mental health unit, but they couldn't see me for another five weeks. Great. The only thing they gave me was a prescription for medication to calm me down, but they wouldn't let me have it until I sobered up. But other than alcohol in my test results, they found small traces of another substance, which required my sample to be sent for further analysis. As yet, I've not been called with the results, and I'm driven to beyond distraction worrying about what they might suggest. My mind races and thoughts bounce around in my mind like a pin-ball machine on crack as I struggle to think about what that substance might be. Did my food get spiked? Alice has made lots of hot drinks for me recently. Did she slip something into one? But surely, I would have tasted something wasn't right if it was in my drink? I can't think straight.

My kids are staying with their granny for their own safety. My mind resembles a tangled bowl of spaghetti; each strand impossible to unravel. How the hell did I get here? Tears well up in my eyes, but I force them back. I need to fix this mess. As I stand there gazing out the window, the eerie silence of the room is deafening. I'm losing myself and I don't know if I have the strength to come back.

It's only eight a.m. and I'm already a blubbering mess, as I wipe away the first tears of the day. I notice a note on the bedside table, scribbled by Greg before he left: "Gone to Mum's to check on the kids. Will be back soon." A sense of tightness grips my chest at the thought of him there with them, without me. I read the note again. There's no softness in his words, not even a kiss at the end. Does he hate me that much?

My phone sits on the table and I check my messages. As I hold it, my vision blurs, and my breathing grows shallow, forcing me to flop back down onto the bed. To clear my brain fog, I follow the A & E doctor's instructions and take a few deep breaths.

But it's no use. I jump up. I need to find Alice.

After throwing on something more presentable, I grab my car keys and with a final deep breath, head for the front door. The crisp autumn air does little to clear my foggy mind; it seems to cloud it further. I slide behind the wheel and start the engine before pulling off the drive. As

I pass the smart houses in our street, I think back to when I loved being here. A quiet, leafy street in a sought-after neighbourhood on the outskirts of Cambridge, and the perfect place to bring up our young family. Now it's tainted with nothing but bad memories that have broken me and my family.

I shake my head as I focus on the road ahead. The journey to Alice's place is a blur of swerving cars and flashing headlights. Horns blare, jolting me back to reality each time I drift off into my dark thoughts.

I pull up to Alice's address. My heart thumps against my ribcage, my palms sweaty, and my T-shirt sticking to my damp armpits. A converted house nestled between two imposing dwellings. It appears serene, yet something feels amiss. I glance round, but the street is quiet, devoid of any signs of life.

"Alright, here goes nothing," I murmur under my breath, stepping out of the car and walking towards the front door. There are two buzzers. Since I know Alice lives on the ground floor, I press the button for her apartment. I hesitate as part of me wants to run back to the safety of my car, but I force myself to stay with every cell of my being on high alert. I step to the side and cup my hands round my eyes as I peer into the lounge. "Alice?" I call out. There's no response, only the rustling of leaves in the breeze behind me.

"Come on, Alice," I plead, knocking on the window with more urgency. When I still receive no answer, I follow the garden path round the side of the property and tap on the kitchen window. Still nothing. I reach for the doorknob, surprised to find it unlocked. With a deep breath, I push the door open and step inside.

"Hello?" I call out, my voice echoing through the empty hallway. "Alice? It's me, Lucy." But only silence greets me, sending shivers through me as I venture further into the apartment, my eyes scanning from left to right.

"Where are you, Alice?"

My thoughts scream at me to turn around and get the hell out of here, but I can't. I need to find her. As I continue my search, each room becomes darker, colder, and more ominous than the last. I move deeper into the apartment, searching each room, unable to shake the nagging sensation that I'm being watched. The silence is deafening as I notice my pulse throbbing in my ears.

"Alice?"

As I round a corner and stop in a doorway, I freeze mid-step and gasp, my eyes fixating on something that sends icy chills down my spine. In the smaller bedroom, the far wall is plastered with pictures of me, all taken from a distance. I can't look away from the unsettling display.

40

LUCY

"Wh-what is this?" I stammer, my body trembling as I step closer to examine the photographs. Confusion roots my body to the spot, my mind trying to piece together why Alice would have these images, and the thought makes me nauseous.

But it's not the photographs of me that grab my attention. Scattered among them are countless press clippings, many of which seem strangely familiar. As I scan the headlines, my eyes widen, and my breath catches in my throat. One particular clipping draws my eyes, detailing the tragic death of a young boy killed by a hit-and-run driver. A sob escapes my lips as I throw a hand over my mouth, unable to take in what I'm seeing. The memory of that day floods back, pain and guilt washing over me.

"God, no," I murmur. The icy chill of dread creeps over me as I think about what twisted connection Alice has to this terrible tragedy.

"Please..." I plead, my eyes darting across the other clippings as I reach for my phone. My hands shake as I take photos. Every headline seems darker, more sinister than the last and it's hard to focus on anything in particular.

"Who are you, Alice?" My voice trembles with fear as I spot a clipping with a picture of a horse-drawn hearse and a crowd of mourners walking behind it. "What do you want with me?" As I stand there, surrounded by the remnants of a terrible tragedy and pictures of me going about my day-to-day life, I feel that I've stumbled into something far more dangerous than I ever could have imagined.

The fine hairs on the back of my neck tickle me as if being stroked. I spin round, half-expecting Alice to be lurking behind me. But there's nothing apart from the eerie silence of the empty apartment. Spooked by my surroundings, I select the photos I've taken and WhatsApp them to Greg. I wait a few seconds. Two black ticks, so I know they've been delivered but Greg's profile also confirms that he's not checked his messages for over an hour. I hit the call button. "Come on, please answer." My call goes through to his voicemail. He must be in a meeting. Shit! I type out another message.

URGENT. I need you at Alice's now. 117, Turner Ave. x

My gaze falls upon a worn diary lying on the crumpled bedcovers. I hesitate for a moment, but curiosity gets the better of me, and I pick it up.

"Jordan..." The name leaps out as I flick through the pages, feeling like an intruder in someone else's most private thoughts. It doesn't take long to realise that this diary is filled with entries about the young boy from the news clippings, chronicling a life cut short. My body tenses as I turn the pages, the enormity of what I'm reading hitting me like a punch to the gut.

"Jesus," I say, staring at the words scrawled in red pen on a page I turn to...

The Perfect Nanny

SHE MUST PAY!!!

As I continue to read, a photo and several more news clippings fall from between the pages of the diary. Sweeping them off the bed, I study the image. It's a boy and girl, both young in age, their faces etched with smiling innocence. A shiver race through me as I connect the dots; they're Jordan and Jessica Albert from the clippings.

"Why me?" My voice cracks with emotion, and I can barely breathe. I was the one who stopped to help Jordan that fateful day, the one who tried to save him. And yet, here I am, years later, caught up in a nightmare not of my making.

Is this some kind of sick joke? Or is this a twisted game?

My brow sweats as I read further passages from the diary. It's clear that Jordan's mother blames the driver for her son's death, and the pain in her words is almost too much to bear as a mother myself. I experience a deep sense of guilt, even though I know I couldn't have saved him.

My phone rings and startles me. The screen tells me it's Greg.

"Luce, what's happened. What are those clippings for?"

With my phone in one hand, and the diary in the other, I fight to get my words out. "Greg, you need to come quick. Alice isn't who she claims to be. I'm sure of that now. She thinks I had something to do with the death of that little boy I told you about. I think she's deranged."

"Lucy, you shouldn't be here."

Alice's voice slices through the air like a knife, and I jump out of my skin as I let out a scream. My fingers lose their grip on my phone and the diary, and both thud to the floor, the diary scattering its secrets round my feet. I turn to face Alice, whose eyes brim with tears.

"Wha... what do you mean?" I stammer, struggling to keep my composure as fear and shock battle for control over my body. My mind conjures up a million plausible explanations for the chilling discoveries I've made within these walls.

"Please, leave my stuff alone. I can explain, though it's the last explanation you'll ever hear." The deadness behind her usually warm eyes, along with her cold, sharp voice send another wave of terror through me. She takes a step forward, her eyes never leaving mine, and I can see the pain etched into every line of her face.

"Explain? How can you explain all of this?" My voice trembles as I flail my arms round the room. I blink back tears, refusing to let them fall in front of her. "You've been following me. Stalking me." I glare at Alice, my eyes wide with fear and anger. "Who are you?" I demand. As I stumble away from Alice, the wall presses against my back, offering no escape. My phone is too far from me, but the call is still connected, so hopefully Greg is still there and listening. I pray he understands the urgency and will be on his way here soon. With the Find My Phone app, he'll know exactly where I am. My accusatory finger trembles as I point it at her, searching for answers hidden behind those fake, innocent brown eyes.

"Lucy, it's not what you think." Tears stream down her face.

"Then tell me the truth." The words spew from my mouth, raw and desperate. I can't contain the turmoil raging inside me any longer. "Why would you have all this?" I gesture to the unsettling collection of photographs and clippings surrounding us.

Alice inhales, steadying herself before speaking. "My

real name isn't Alice Simpson," she admits, her gaze locked on mine. "It's Jessica Albert. I changed it years ago after..." She pauses, choking on her words. "After Jordan died."

"Jordan... your brother?" I struggle to keep the shock out of my voice, trying to piece together the fragments of truth that seem to shatter my world even more.

"Yes." Her voice cracks as she continues. "I was so lost after he died. I couldn't face the memories, the heartache. So, I ran away from it all and created a new life as Alice. That's why you couldn't find anything about me before the age of eighteen. I had to wait until then to legally change my name."

"Is that why you're keeping these? To hold onto him?" I ask, unable to suppress the curiosity that twists at my gut despite the sheer dread smothering me.

"Partly," she admits, wiping away her tears with the back of her hand. "But there's more to it than that. These were a constant reminder of what happened to Jordan, the tragedy that changed everything in my life. I needed to remember, to make sure I never forgot."

"Forgot what?" I hiss, my patience wearing thin as I struggle to comprehend the enormity of it all.

"Lucy, shut up, please," she begs, her eyes fiery and angry.

"Then tell me!" My scream echoes through the small room, bouncing off the walls.

"You're a killer," she screams. Alice's accusation stings. The words leave me breathless while I wrestle to make sense of her accusation. I know I'm unravelling amidst the chaos.

"Look," I plead, my voice shaking, "I don't know what you think you know, but I'm not a killer." I want to believe my own words, to push away the doubts creeping into the corners of my mind, but something in Alice's eyes makes it impossible.

"Lucy, understand... I've been living with this pain for years. It's consumed me, made me question everything about my life and who I am. And now that I've found you, I need answers and I need you to pay for what you did."

"A... answers? What answers could I give you? What did I do?" I stutter, my confusion growing by the second.

"About Jordan and how he died. How you were involved." That last word hangs in the air between us, her eyes never leaving mine.

"Involved? I didn't kill anyone. I tried to help him, but it was too late."

"Then why did you drive off?" Alice challenges. "You acted as if nothing had happened and carried on with your life. You got married and started a family. And yet, what did you leave me? Broken-hearted because you took the life of my brother."

"I didn't drive off. I stopped to help. To help both of you."

Alice's voice is cold and distant, her eyes devoid of any warmth. "You left him there to die."

"Please," I implore, my hands trembling as I reach out to her.

"You lie. You killed my brother." As Alice speaks she pulls a knife from behind her back, the blade glinting in the light. My eyes widen in horror.

"Alice. Put the knife down. We can talk about this, work through it together. There's still hope for us, and for you," I beg as the room spins round me.

"Hope? There's no hope left for either of us, Lucy. Not after everything that's happened. This has consumed me for so many years, it's become my identity. I've done my best to make you suffer. To bring you to your knees. I should have put more in your wine to cripple you and make you brain-dead." The weapon never wavers in her hand.

My eyes narrow as I process her words. Wine. Cripple. Brain-dead. Alice spiked my wine? I should have known. "There's no need for this. We can make it right."

"Make it right? How can anything be right again after what you've done?" she spits out, the knife quivering in her grip.

I sense a panic attack coming as my knees weaken and sweat beads on my forehead. "I'm so sorry. But we can't change the past. All we can do now is try to move forward and heal."

"Move forward? You think you can waltz through life unscathed while my brother's memory fades into nothing? You think I'll let you forget?" She sneers, her face twisted with rage.

"Of course not. I would never forget Jordan, I promise. And I want to help you heal, too. Maybe we can find some sort of... I don't know, closure together?" I blurt out, trying to reason with her and stall.

Alice's laugh is bitter and hollow. "There is no closure for a mother who's lost her child. A sister who has lost her brother never finds closure either. Nothing exists except pain. And you deserve every bit of misery you've had over recent weeks. And I want it to last longer. To be even more severe. Your suffering is the only thing that eases my agony."

Tears burn my eyes. "I know I can never understand your pain, but please, let me try to help you. You can't keep living like this, consumed by darkness and grief."

"The one and only thing that would help me is if you could bring my brother back. And since that's impossible, all I have left is to put you through the same agony I've been living with!" she screams, the knife still close.

"Don't do this." My body trembles as I take a slow, cautious step towards her.

"Stay back!" she shrieks, jabbing the knife forward and waving it. "You don't get to come any closer."

"Okay, okay," I relent, stepping back, my hands raised, palms out. "I won't come any closer. Please put the knife down. Can we not talk about this rationally?"

Alice's laughter carries a tinge of madness. "What's rational about a world where they rip innocent children away from their families while letting the responsible ones walk free?"

"We're both drowning here. If you go through with this and allow this hatred and despair to swallow you up, it will leave nothing but emptiness. Please, let me help you find a way out."

For a moment, it seems she might waver. Her grip on the knife loosens, and her eyes once cold and hard as stone, soften with unshed tears.

But then, in an instant, her fury returns, fiercer and more terrifying than before.

41

LUCY

ALICE'S EYES ARE WILD, her hair dishevelled, each strand framing her face like a shadowy halo. Her voice slices through the silence with shocking effect.

"Lucy, I know you killed my brother."

Shock ripples through me, churning my insides. The words make little sense. They are not true. "Wh-what? I didn't kill your brother. I would never hurt anyone, you know that." I watch Alice battle with the anger within her. I've always known Alice to be gentle and reserved, but something else seems to have taken control of her. Something much darker, sinister, and terrifying.

"We're friends. Listen to what I have to say."

Alice's eyes flicker with uncertainty for a moment.

"Your brother..." I begin, searching for the right words. "I didn't kill him. I swear it. There must be some kind of misunderstanding, or maybe someone's trying to set me up. But it wasn't me."

For a long moment, Alice stares at me, her dark eyes boring into mine, as if she's trying to decipher the truth. It's all I can do to hold her gaze.

"There's nothing you can say that will make a scrap of difference."

"Fine. Your brother's death wasn't my fault. He was lying in the road after being hit by another car, and I found him. I tried to help." My hands tremble as I recall the harrowing scene.

"You mean you left him there to die and drove off?" Alice replies, spittle flying from her lips.

"No!" I shout, desperate to make her understand. "I called for help and stayed with both of you until the ambulance arrived. I'm so sorry."

Alice reaches down and grabs my phone. Her face contorts as she checks the screen and sees Greg's name. She looks at me for a second and bares her teeth before disconnecting the call. "You won't need this anymore." Alice stuffs my phone into the pocket of her hoodie. Despite the fear tightening every muscle, a sliver of hope breaks through. Even though I don't have my phone, Greg will still be able to track my location as long as Alice keeps it on her person. "Sorry? That's all you have to say. My brother is dead because of you."

The sudden force of Alice's scream cuts through the air like a lightning bolt, shattering the fragile peace between us. "Enough!" she shouts, her voice raw with anger and desperation. "We're going on a little drive together. You and me. And you'll do as I say, or else you'll die a very bloody death right here." She steps towards me and prods the tip of the knife into my side.

I gasp, the sharp edge of the blade digging through the fabric of my clothes and into my skin.

"Get your keys," she demands, her eyes dark and unreadable as she grips the weapon tighter. I fumble for my keys, trying to keep my hands steady. We leave the apartment in silence, the tension between us leaving us both rigid. For her it's anger, but for me it's fear.

As soon as we're inside the car, Alice directs me towards the edge of the city. My thoughts fly at a million miles an hour as I wonder how to defuse this volatile situation. I have no idea where the nearest police station is, nor can I think of braking and getting out, the knife still touching my skin.

"Drive faster!" Alice shouts, her gaze locked on the winding country lanes that stretch out before us.

"Please, I don't want to die. Think of what Matthew and Sarah will go through if they lose their mummy?"

"Shut up and drive," she hisses, ignoring my pleas. The knife digs deeper into my side, forcing me to stifle a cry of pain. With no choice, I press my foot down on the accelerator, and the car lurches forward, picking up speed as it hurtles round the tight bends. The once familiar and picturesque landscape now seems like a terrifying racetrack. The car roars as I push it to the limit, my hands gripping the wheel so hard that my knuckles hurt.

My phone pings inside Alice's hoodie. She reaches for it and reads out the message.

"On my way. Called the police. Be careful."

"Bit late for your knight in shining armour to save you. This will all be over in a few minutes." Alice tosses the phone onto the back seat.

"Is this what you want? What will this prove?" I shout.

"Shut up. Faster."

As we continue our reckless journey through the countryside, I realise that there may be no way out of this nightmare. Every plea and attempt at reasoning with Alice does little to change her view and her thirst for vengeance. I have no choice but to drive faster, praying that I can bring us both back from the brink before it's too late. The cold steel of the knife presses harder against my side in response as Alice leans in close, her breath hot in my ear. I feel a wetness forming between my legs as fear tightens my insides.

"Drive faster," she orders, her voice calm amidst the chaos. "We're going to re-enact the hit-and-run that killed my brother, and you're going to feel every agonising second of it."

"Is this what your brother would want? Would he want you to hurt me like this?" I try to reason with her, even though I know it's a long shot. Alice seems too far gone to be rational.

"You know shit about him, or what he'd want. This is about justice. Floor it. You owe me this! You owe my brother this!" she screams like a wounded wild animal.

As much as I try to keep my wits about me, there's no denying the gnawing fear that twists my gut. And yet, somewhere beneath my fear, a seed of determination takes root. I refuse to let this be my end. I glance over at her, searching for any hint of humanity behind those dark eyes. She's lost, consumed by grief and rage.

"Alright." My grip tightens as my foot presses down on the accelerator, the engine screaming beneath the bonnet. The car surges forward, the world outside a blur.

"More!" she shouts.

The tyres screech against the tarmac as I swerve round another sharp bend, the knife pressing deeper into my side as a cold reminder.

I'm trying to tamp down my pain and terror when a pothole hidden close to the grassy verge catches the front wheel. To my surprised gasp, the car lurches violently to one side. I struggle to regain control, but it's too late. The vehicle spins off the road and flips over, before crashing into a ditch with a sickening crunch. Silence follows. The world looks different. My vision swims, disorientated by the impact, and pain flares through my body. Survival mode kicks in as I smell petrol. I don't want to die in a fireball if the car goes up. With every ounce of strength I have left, I claw my way out of the wreckage through my broken side window. The acrid smell of burning rubber fills my nostrils. I crawl away across the dirt, my body screaming in pain.

"Lucy." Alice's voice is shrill and desperate, a far cry from her recent fury. She staggers out of the car on her side, her face contorted with pain and confusion as she searches for the knife that has slipped from her grasp. Blood trickles down her face from a head injury.

"Stay away from me," I warn her, struggling to find my footing on the uneven ground.

"I'm going to kill you," she spits, her eyes wild with rage. Her gaze flickers between me and the mangled wreck of the car. "Where's the bloody knife?" Her hands claw at the ground in desperation. "I need to finish this."

"NO!" I yell, lunging forward to tackle her to the ground. Our bodies collide, and we struggle against one another, each fighting for our own survival. All my fear, anger, and heartache pour into the fight, fuelled by the hope that somehow I might make it out of this alive. But I don't know how long I can fight her off. I can't hear any sirens and I only hope that Greg can get here soon. With my phone in the car, he'll know where I am. *Please, Greg, hurry up.*

But as our limbs tangle and each of us claw at one another, I know there can only be one survivor as I see the first flames flicker from the front of the car. Alice pushes me back down and sits astride of me, wrapping her hands round my neck. Her grip tightens. My throat closes and my eyes bulge as speckles of black fill my vision. The car is going to explode at any moment and if I don't get away, then I'll die in the flames along with Alice. And so, with every fibre of my being, I fight on for my life as my hand curls into a fist and I punch her in the face.

42

ALICE

THE PAIN SEARS through my face as I reel from Lucy's unexpected punch. She shoves me away, sending me falling to the ground. I clutch at my throbbing nose, feeling the warm blood stream between my fingers. Bitch.

"Help. Somebody, please help me," Lucy's voice cracks as she stumbles to her feet, coughing and spluttering. Her eyes are wild with fear, and her once-neat blonde hair is a tangled mess.

I can't let her get away. With every ounce of strength left in me, I push myself up and go after her. She can scream as much as she wants. We're surrounded by nothing but fields and the odd isolated farm building.

"Please, Alice," she sobs, hobbling away from me. "Why are you doing this?"

"Shut up," I snarl, my bloodied hair clinging to my face as I close the gap between us, spurred on by the end in sight.

Lucy's slender frame trembles, her clothes now dirty and torn as she tries to get away, with flailing arms, clawing at the empty air for something to hold onto, anything to keep her from falling.

"Stay away from me!" she screams, stumbling over the uneven ground pitted with wide tyre marks where farm vehicles have passed over recent days. I can almost feel her panic, her confusion, like it's my own. But there's no going back now.

"You're dead!" I scream.

"Please, Alice... I don't want to die..." she pleads.

"Neither did Jordan," I hiss, my eyes narrowing as I remember the brother I lost all those years ago.

Her lower lip trembles, which only makes me hate her more. "But that was an accident..."

"Shut up!" I shout as I close the gap and lunge for her, grabbing hold of her hair.

She howls as she clutches the sides of her head. "Let go of me!" she screeches, tears streaming down her cheeks.

"No!" I roar, yanking her back and forcing her to the ground. I won't let her go this time. As we exchange punches and scratches, our bodies writhe in the dirt. Our stained, torn, and bloodied clothes hanging from us in tatters.

Lucy drags her nails down my face, leaving trails of hot, stinging pain that only fuel my rage. I scream, possessed by my demons that have simmered beneath the surface for so long. My eyes widen and I bare my teeth, spittle flying from my lips as I search the ground for something to finish this. My hand closes round a rock, its jagged edges digging into my palm. Without hesitation, I smash it against Lucy's temple, dazing her. I thought she'd scream, but she moans, her eyes rolling back as her body goes limp. But I can't stop now. I raise the rock and swing it back down again several times, rendering her motionless.

Tossing the rock aside, I straddle Lucy, my hands wrapping round her throat once more. My fingers dig into her soft flesh, desperate to finish her. Anger, sadness, and fear race through my mind at a hundred miles an hour, blurring my vision. The red mist descends. Everything I've worked for, all the planning, scheming, and fake niceness has led me to this moment. Revenge for Jordan and retribution for Lucy.

I hear a voice. And it takes a moment for me to regain my senses as I realise Lucy has come around. "Please... Alice..." she croaks under the pressure of my grip. But I ignore her. I squeeze harder, my knuckles whitening as her breaths become more laboured.

"Jordan deserved better." My voice trembles with emotion. "And so do I."

As Lucy's struggles fade and her body weakens, my thoughts turn inward, consumed by memories of Jordan and the life we once shared. The guilt and pain of losing him threatens to swallow me whole, but that won't bring him back. It won't change anything.

"You deserve to suffer in hell, Lucy," I murmur, tightening my grip one last time.

I blink, my vision blurred by a heady mix of rage and tears. The voices inside of me grow louder as each second passes. As I shut my eyes for a moment, I'm transported to our garden where a younger me and Jordan were locked in an argument.

"Give it back," I snarl, my hands balled into fists by my sides.

But Jordan smirks, waving my beloved book above his head. "Make me," he taunts, dancing away from my reach.

"Jordan. Please," I scream, frustration twisting at my insides. The more I struggle to reach it, the further away he seems to get, his laughter growing fainter with each step.

"Come on, Alice. Can't catch me?" he taunts, his cruel smile crushing as he darts away from me.

"Jordan, please..." I plead, out of breath and gasping. I chase after him, my hair whipping round my face and my old-fashioned dress billowing behind me. "You're so horrible. I wish you'd die."

The words leave my lips before I can even think of taking them back. A sharp pang of guilt crushes my chest. The sound of an engine revving in the distance catches my attention, and fear grips me.

"Jordan!" I scream, my eyes widening with terror as I notice the car flying towards us. I can feel my body tense, urging me to run faster, to reach him before time runs out. But there's nothing I can do to slow down time. "Jordan, watch out!" I shriek, desperation lacing my voice. But my warning comes too late; the car barrels into him as he races out into the road. Jordan's small body arcs through the air like a flimsy rag doll, limbs flailing. The sickening crunch of shattering bones leaves me frozen in place.

"JORDAN!" The scream rips from my throat, raw and primal, but the driver stops for a moment and then pulls away before disappearing.

"NO!" I cry, my legs unfreezing as I rush towards his twisted, broken body sprawled across the ground. I can't breathe, can't think; my heart pounding against the iron cage of my ribs. Hot tears stream down my cheeks, blurring the scene before me. I'm at a loss for what to do as I fall to my knees and cradle his limp hand in mine, the warmth fading as I say desperate apologies. I shake his shoulders, desperate for him to wake. I push back an eyelid, hoping he'll wake and look at me. As I lift his head, blood pools beneath it and sticks to my fingers. "Please, wake up." But there's nothing.

"Please forgive me, Jordan. Please wake up. I didn't mean it," I say through the sobs that wrack my body. The world round me seems to collapse, leaving only the crushing weight of grief and guilt paralysing my body.

"Let me help you, sweetie," says a woman, her arm slipping round my waist, trying to coax me away. I notice her car close to Jordan. Her soft voice is like a lifeline as my mind spins out of control.

"NO!" I scream, my nails digging into Jordan's lifeless hand, refusing to let go. "I'm not leaving him."

The woman's arms tighten round me, offering comfort amidst the devastation.

"Stay with me," the woman implores, her voice sounding distant and faint. But I can't. My legs give way, and I collapse into her arms.

"Jordan..." His name is literally torn from my body, my heart heavy with a grief that will never fade. I look up at the woman comforting me.

The scene fades away, replaced by the cold, unforgiving reality of the present. I gasp. Horror fills my eyes as the darkest part of my subconscious mind reveals the final missing pieces of the jigsaw. The arm round me... it was Lucy's. She stopped to help *after* the hit-and-run driver had sped away. She wasn't the speeding driver who killed Jordan.

And just like that, I'm pulled back into the present moment, my hands still wrapped round Lucy's throat. I fall to one side as heat cuts through me, my mind swirling, sweat dripping off my forehead, my bowels twitching. The sound of tyres screeching close by and the distant wail of sirens fractures the silence. I hear Lucy's name being called and Greg's familiar voice. I stare at the clouds floating past. The calmness above soothes my pain as my vision darkens and I pass out.

43

GREG

I can't catch my breath as I rush to Lucy to find her body lifeless, bloodied, and bruised. "Please, God, no. No." I drop to my knees as a swell of panic consumes my body like a tsunami. I feel sick as my stomach turns. She looks so fragile and broken that I'm scared to touch her. I hear the sirens closing in and I know help is moments away.

"Hang in there, darling. You're going to be okay; help is coming." I gently push her damp hair away from her forehead and feel the stickiness coat my fingers. My eyes widen in horror. Blood. A small crimson river trickles out of a deep gash beneath her hairline. Her blonde hair now spattered pink and her skin more blush than it ever was before. "Oh Jesus, what has she done to you?"

I take Lucy's hand in mind as tears blur my vision. I'm so lost in grief and worry that I don't hear approaching footsteps until moments later.

My heart racing with each step, I rush through the hospital doors searching for someone to talk to at the reception desk in A & E. The last time I was here was to get help for Lucy. And now I'm back again hoping that Lucy will survive. While paramedics worked to stabilise Luce during the journey to the hospital, the police escorted me here and promised to fetch my car later. Nodding to the officers, I express my gratitude for their service and slap my hands on the desk. Even in this state of dreading what I might find, I'm aware of the sterile smell that fills the air, a scent that makes my stomach churn.

"Please. I need to see Lucy Butler. She's my wife," I beg the triage nurse, my voice shaking.

"Of course." The male nurse checks his screen and tells me to head down the corridor, and it's the last cubicle.

My legs feel heavy as I sprint down the hallway, barely keeping myself upright. The flickering fluorescent lights above only add to the surreal nightmare I find myself in. I reach the final cubicle, and my heart nearly stops.

Lucy lies twisted amidst a tangle of wires and tubes, her slender body battered and bruised. Her once-lively eyes are closed, and her long blonde hair is matted with blood and dirt, a stark contrast against the crisp white sheets.

"Oh God, Lucy." My voice cracks as I choke back further tears.

"Mr Butler?" A firm but compassionate voice says. I turn to face a doctor in scrubs. "I'm Dr Taylor. We're doing everything we can for your wife. She's lost a lot of blood, but her vitals are stable. Mrs Butler suffered a deep hairline fracture to her skull. There's a slight swelling on her brain, and there's extensive bruising to the tissue of her neck."

"Thank you." My throat constricts with emotion as my eyes fill with tears. "Will she be okay?"

Dr Taylor offers a small smile. "Its early days, but we're hopeful. We'll run further scans on her injuries now that she's stable. Our focus needs to be on monitoring the swelling in her brain. I was reviewing her blood test results from her recent visit. The lab found traces of zopiclone. But there's nothing in her medical records of her being prescribed the medication for insomnia."

"She never was as far as I'm aware. Why would she have them?"

"I don't know, Mr Butler, but we'll need to liaise with your GP. But there was enough to suggest it had been in her system for a while. And without proper supervision it can lead to extreme side effects in certain people."

"Such as?"

"Serious side effects are poor memory, hallucinations, delusions, and depression."

I gasp as the realisation sinks in. The changes in Lucy's behaviour. Dear God, she was right all along. Alice must have spiked her drinks or food.

I grip the side of the bed to steady myself as a wave of relief washes over me. But that's quickly followed by a larger wave of guilt. How could I not have seen it? How could I not have believed my wife? I thank the doctor before he leaves. So much of me wants to rush to the room further down where I know the police are holding Alice. In comparison, her injuries are insignificant, and the police have handcuffed her to a bedside rail. I need answers. I demand answers. I need to look her in the eyes and hear why she's done this to my Lucy.

I take my wife's hand in mine, my thumb rubbing the back of her soft skin. "I don't know how we got here, but I'm so sorry for not believing you. Please forgive me. I'll make this right. I promise." Unshed tears blur my vision.

As if on cue, another doctor enters the room. He's an older gentleman, with a kind yet weary face that suggests he's seen it all. He introduces himself as Dr Scott and I recognise his name right away.

"Mr Butler," he begins. "I'm sorry for the dreadful experience Lucy has been through. I believe I can shed some light on her situation."

"Go on," I reply hesitantly, my grip on Lucy's hand tightening.

"Years ago, when Alice was younger, someone killed her brother Jordan in a hit-and-run accident," he explains, his voice gentle. "The event severely traumatised Alice and as a result, she developed repressed memory syndrome. When the trauma experienced is too severe to be kept in conscious memory, individuals may develop repressed memory syndrome through repression or dissociation, or both. Later it may be recalled, often under certain circumstances, and reappear in conscious memory, sometimes all in one go, or as a series of incomplete flashbacks. Alice's mind blocked out most of the details surrounding her brother's death to protect her from the terrible pain she felt. It was a natural self-protection mechanism to allow her to continue with life."

I struggle to comprehend what he's saying. "And how does Lucy fit into all of this?"

"Lucy was the first person Alice saw after the accident. Because of her trauma, instead of blaming the unknown driver who killed Jordan, Alice's subconscious laid the blame on the first person it saw, in this case, Lucy. She couldn't process her own guilt for chasing her brother and it being her fault that he ran into the road. Alice could not save her brother, so she needed someone else to bear the burden of her guilt. Someone else to blame."

"Are you saying she's been harbouring this resentment for years?"

"Yes. Her behaviour has shown that she never recovered from the trauma. Something triggered these repressed memories and emotions to resurface, causing her to find Lucy and make her pay."

"Jesus Christ," I mutter, my head spinning. As much as I hate Alice for hurting Lucy, I have a sense of pity for her. The burden of the guilt must have been unbearable for a child.

"Thank you, Dr Scott. I appreciate your insight."

The man nods as his gaze sweeps over my seriously injured wife. "Of course, Mr Butler. I'm truly sorry for what your family is going through."

As Dr Scott steps back to give me space. I sit in the dim hospital light, holding onto Lucy's hand as if it's a lifeline. I vow to stay by her side until she's recovered, and to do everything in my power to make sure that Alice faces justice for the pain she's caused us. My jaw clenches as anger swells inside of me for not trusting Lucy's instincts. She knew something was off about Alice, sensing the danger. But I dismissed her fears, blinded by my own stubborn need for a rational explanation. My behaviour was deplorable. And not just since we hired Alice. From long before that. I have a lot of making up to do to become the best husband and father I can be.

I glance over my shoulder to find Dr Scott still standing there with a pinched expression. "Lucy warned me. She said Alice was dangerous, but I didn't listen. I thought she was being paranoid. Shit."

"It's not your fault. Repressed memories can be unpredictable and volatile. There's no way you could've expected this happening."

"Still, I should've trusted my wife," I say, clenching my fist.

"From what I've gathered so far Alice likely snapped under the pressure of the resurfacing memories during a moment of intense emotion. Her violence came from a place of deep rooted psychological anguish."

"Will Alice get better? Will she be able to face legal proceedings? I want... We need justice," I ask, trying to find hope in this nightmare.

"Recovery is possible, but it will be a long and difficult journey. It's impossible to predict how much progress she'll make, how damaged she is, or whether she'll ever be able to fully come to terms with her past. Right now, our focus should be on helping Lucy heal."

"Of course." I look back at Lucy's fragile form on the hospital bed, her chest rising and falling with each shallow breath. Her hand, still in mine, was cold and weak. I need her to recover; I need her strength, her laughter, her love... and her forgiveness. "Thank you, Dr Scott." My throat tightens with emotion before he leaves me alone with Lucy.

My own stupid and selfish failings bears down on me. It wasn't Alice's fractured psyche that brought us here; it was my failure to listen, to trust in the woman I love. "Lucy, I'm so sorry I didn't believe you. I promise you, from now on, I'll always listen. We'll get through this."

The monotonous beep of the heart monitor fills the silence. The room feels claustrophobic.

"Mr Butler?" A nurse peeks into the room. "Would you like a tea or coffee?"

"Thank you, but no," I reply, wiping away my tears. "I want to stay here with Lucy."

"Of course. Let me know if you need anything." She gives me a small, understanding smile before leaving me alone once more.

I turn back to Lucy, her features so still and fragile as I recognise how close I came to losing her because of Alice's deranged breakdown. "Please come back to me, Luce." I grip her hand, trying to will her awake. But she remains unresponsive, the rhythmic beeping of the machine her only response.

ONCE SHE'S ON A WARD, days meld into nights, time becoming a blur as I maintain my vigil at Lucy's bedside. I pray for the first time in years, bargaining with whatever higher power there may be to bring her back to me. "God, if you're listening," I murmur one evening, "please let her wake up. She doesn't deserve this."

As the days pass, Lucy's condition slowly stabilises further, and a cautious hope grows within me. The doctors say they cannot predict when she'll regain consciousness, but each small sign of progress is a step in the right direction. The blows to her brain led to extensive swelling and the state of unconsciousness. Though not life threatening, doctors monitored her and allowed her body to repair itself. A knife wound needed stitches and a cracked rib will heal by itself. I've spent hours staring at her bruised and battered face wondering how it's ended up like that. What signs did I miss? What could I have done differently? The guilt gnaws away at my insides like a hungry rat.

The kids are staying with my mum. I've told them they're on a mini holiday which excited them. I don't want to bring them here. It would break their hearts to see their mummy looking like this. But I keep praying for the day when Lucy's eyes will open once more, and we can heal as a family.

44

GREG

Three Days Later...

The smell of burnt coffee fills my nostrils as I pace the kitchen this afternoon waiting to head back to the hospital. Despite being told by the nursing staff to stay home and get a good night's sleep, I'm desperate to get back to my wife's side.

"Greg," Beth's voice startles me from my thoughts. She enters the kitchen, carrying a steaming casserole dish. "You need to eat something later."

"Thanks, Beth. That's really kind of you," I mumble.

"Any news?" Beth sets the dish on the table.

"Nothing yet."

Beth nods, pouring a cuppa for herself, before coming to stand alongside of me. She rubs my back and stares at me. "Greg, you're not alone in this. We're all here for you. The neighbours ask for an update every day. Betty and David at number eleven asked if there's anything they could do to help. Though I'm not sure what, as they're both in their eighties," Beth laughs, trying to lighten the mood.

Her touch brings jolts me, and I laugh. "Thank you. I appreciate it. Say thank you from me."

"Of course. Now, please, eat something. Can I make you some bacon and scrambled eggs? You can have the casserole this evening. Lucy wouldn't want you to waste away worrying about her."

I turn to her, my appetite non-existent. My mind races with unanswered questions, replaying the events leading up to Alice's twisted actions. "Why? How did we miss the signs?"

"Greg. You can't blame yourself for what happened. None of us saw it coming. Alice seemed so normal. She was so great with the kids."

"Maybe I never saw it coming," I concede, clenching my fists. "But I should have listened to Lucy. I should have believed her when she told me something was off."

"Lucy is strong. She's a tough old boot. I feel as bad for not believing her. I'm her best friend and annoying neighbour. We've all made mistakes. She'll make it through this," Beth reassures me as she lets out a sigh.

As the afternoon wears on, more neighbours stop by, offering food, consolation, and words of encouragement. But their well-meaning gestures do little to lighten my mood. What if my wife never regains consciousness? I can barely stomach the thought of it.

Because it would be my fault.

THREE TORTUROUS DAYS PASS, and once again I sit beside Lucy's hospital bed. The rhythmic sound of the machines monitoring her vital signs does little to ease my worry. I hold her hand, welcoming the warmth of her skin. "Come on, Lucy. You're a fighter." My voice breaks as I lay my head on her bed. "I need you."

I shut my eyelids and drift away for a few minutes before I'm jolted awake by a voice.

"Greg?" she murmurs.

"Lucy. Oh, thank God!" I bolt upright, tears filling my eyes as I squeeze her hand and reach for the call button to alert the nurses.

She squeezes my hand in response, her own eyes filling with tears.

"Lucy, keep fighting. You're doing amazing. You'll be home before you know it." As I sit there offering words of encouragement, I realise she is my rock, the one person who keeps me grounded when everything else seems to fall apart.

"Ta," she says, her voice conveying a mixture of exhaustion and gratitude as a nurse arrives followed by a doctor.

The sterile scent of the hospital room, mixed with the lingering odour of disinfectant and the hot food trolley outside, assaults my senses as I watch Lucy's chest rise and fall in a steady rhythm as the doctor checks her vitals. The steady beep of the heart monitor has become a constant companion during these long hours spent waiting for this moment.

"Are... are the kids okay?" she asks, struggling to form the words.

"Luce, they are," I answer without hesitation, squeezing her hand for reassurance.

"Promise me, Greg... promise me you'll always believe me from now on," she pleads, her vulnerability laid bare as she stares at the ceiling.

"I promise." My eyelids flutter as I struggle to hold back my own tears. "I seriously messed up and I'm sorry for doubting you. I should have trusted you. From now on, I will. Always."

She turns her head and winces as her eyes search mine. Our gazes lock, and for a moment, it's as if nothing else exists but the two of us, suspended in time. The noise of conversations in the corridor, the clatter of the food trolley, the phones ringing at the nurses' desk, they all fade out to nothing.

45

LUCY

A Few Weeks Later...

Fluffy white clouds roll by through the lounge window. I sit on the sofa, a throw draped over my legs. There's not a drop of alcohol in the house, my decision. It's a relief that I don't need or crave a drop at all. It's been a few weeks since that dreadful day, and I'm here, healing day by day surrounded by my loving family. Their support is like a warm embrace, comforting me during these challenging times. My sister Jill came over from Wales to see me and my parents travelled from Lincolnshire and stayed in a local Premier Inn so they could see me and take care of the kids for a few days. I still recall the look of shock and sadness etched on my dad's features. In his eyes, I've always been his 'little girl' and seeing the tears cascade down his face only saddened me.

"Luce, do you want your cuppa?" Greg asks as he enters the room, a warm smile on his face. He's been catering to my every need, making up for lost time.

"Thank you." I shift on the sofa to sit more upright. As he disappears into the kitchen, I think about how much has changed between us. Our conversations are now laced with openness, vulnerability, and a renewed understanding.

"Here you go." Greg hands me a mug of tea. As I take it from him, our fingers brush against each other, and I love that connection.

"Thanks," I say. "You know, you don't have to take care of everything round here."

"Luce, I owe it to you, and besides, it's doctor's orders that you have to rest as much as you can." He takes a seat beside me and stares at me with a childlike grin that makes me chuckle.

"Greg, you'll have to get back to the office eventually, and do a full day's work." As I place my hand on his cheek, he leans into my touch, closing his eyes before pulling away.

"Well, it's my company, so I can hardly fire myself," he laughs, rolling his eyes. I take a sip of my tea, enjoying its warmth soothing my throat.

"I promise to always be there for you, Luce. You and the kids are my world. How about a holiday to Dubai? All-inclusive, five-star. All four of us, or just you and me. Mum can have the kids for a week?"

I smile. A tear rolls down my cheek as I think about the love he holds for us. As we sit there, sipping our tea, the weight of the past seems to lift ever so slightly. And for now, that's enough for me.

The doorbell rings, and Greg stands up to answer it. "I bet that's Beth," he says, a smile in his voice. I hear him greet her at the door as I take another sip of my tea.

"Lucy," Beth calls out, her voice like sunshine breaking through the clouds. She strides into the lounge with another bouquet cradled in her arms. "These are for you."

"Thank you, Beth. You don't have to. This is your

fourth bouquet." My friend smothers me in a warm hug. The scent of the flowers fills the room, their vibrant colours lifting my spirits. I watch as Greg takes them from her and arranges them in a vase, adding to the collection of cards and flowers from friends that have been brightening our home.

"Kids are playing upstairs," Greg says, knowing that Beth loves spending time with Matthew and Sarah. "Why don't you go and cheer them up?"

"Sounds like a plan," Beth replies, as she marches back out of the lounge and thunders up the stairs heavy-footed to wind me up. The sound of her laughter soon mixes with the children's giggles.

"She's been such a help these past few weeks," I say, touched by her unwavering support and love. He nods, placing the vase on the deep windowsill because the coffee table is already chocka with other floral displays.

"I don't know what we would've done without her." His tone is sincere as he sits back down next to me.

We sit in silence for a moment, listening to the sounds of silly screams, shouts, and laughter coming from upstairs. It's a stark contrast to the tense atmosphere that filled our home a few weeks ago.

"Things will get better," Greg says, as if reading my thoughts. "And I'll be here every step of the way."

I have to agree with him. I've been getting better by the day. My body is healing, the headaches aren't as intense, and the therapy sessions have helped me to sort out my head and my feelings. I think back to my first session when things were so raw. I sat, picking at the hem of my blouse as I recalled the harrowing events surrounding Alice's violent obsession. My therapist, Dr Patel, stressed the importance of allowing myself the grace and space to process the emotions, as suppression would only breed more anxiety. With his patience and gentle prompts, each session became easier, and it felt like a heavy cloak was being lifted from me.

Dr Patel and Dr Scott have both echoed the reminder that Alice's actions reflected her own inner turmoil. As our sessions progressed over the weeks, I found solace in the safe space created by my therapy. My thoughts became untangled with Dr Patel's help, and I understood the depths of Alice's fixation and how I had become the target of her displaced emotions.

As night falls, I find myself drawn to my bedroom window, my gaze sweeping across the garden and into the woods beyond, searching for any sign of movement among the trees. The darkness spawns my fears, and my mind still plays tricks on me.

"Lucy, come back downstairs," Greg calls from the doorway, his voice laced with concern. I pull away from the window, the cold glass leaving a chill on my fingertips as I step back.

"Alright." Worry lines crease my forehead. "I'm coming."

He wraps his arms round me in the doorway, pulling me into a warm embrace. "You're safe now, Luce. We all are. Alice can't hurt us anymore."

I nod against his chest, but the knot in my stomach remains. "I know." Though I glance back at the window one last time before we leave, wondering if there are shadows that glide between the trees.

"Lucy." Greg sits down beside me on the sofa. His warm hand finds mine beneath the blanket, fingers intertwining. "You're safe now. I've installed a state-of-the-art security system, with cameras and motion sensors covering every inch of the garden. If anything or anyone comes near this house, we'll know about it."

I know he's doing his best to make us safe again, and I appreciate it more than I can put into words. But the fear lingers.

"Luce, let's talk about your plans for getting back to work."

We settle back on the sofa, my legs resting on the pouffe as I lean into Greg's embrace, grateful for the distraction. "Beth wants to look after Matthew and Sarah three days a week because she works from home. It would be such a relief knowing they're in good hands."

Greg agrees. "That's a great idea. And Mum is always eager to spend more time with her grandchildren. She can help on the other two days."

"Exactly," I reply, my spirits lifting at the thought. "It's a perfect arrangement. It'll give me the chance to ease back into work without worrying about the kids, and I'll be working the odd day from home anyway."

"Then it's settled." He plants a soft kiss on my cheek. "We'll do whatever it takes to get you back on your feet. One day at a time."

As we talk about my return to work, I sense the swell of determination rise within me. I've survived the darkness of Alice's obsession, and now it's time to get my life back.

46

DR SCOTT

THE STERILE WHITE walls of the psychiatric hospital rinse any human emotion from the corridor as I watch Jessica through the small window in her door. She sits motionless, staring at the dull plaster, lost in a world of her own. I push open the door, my footsteps echoing through the silence.

"Morning, Jessica. It's Dr Scott here," I say, as a nurse lingers in the doorway for my safety.

She doesn't respond, her hair falling like a curtain round her pinched face. Her brown eyes stay fixated on the wall, as if she's searching for an answer etched into its cold surface.

My thoughts drift back to the accident, and I feel a chill in my spine. I know her tormented memories continue going through her mind, refusing to relent. Jessica feels she was responsible for Jordan's death, and after all these years, the truth could no longer stay buried. It clawed its way to the surface, tearing apart her reality.

As I watch Jessica, I recall the reason it's come to this.

The moment Lucy appeared, mere seconds after the accident, her fate was sealed. I'd stopped for a moment further down the road and saw Lucy step from her car and run to Jessica. In her desperation to protect herself, Jessica's mind distorted her experience, superimposing her guilt for Jordan's death on Lucy. And now she's trapped in this self-inflicted prison.

"Talk to me, Jessica," I say. "Tell me what you're thinking."

Her lips part slightly, as if she's considering my request, but then close, sealing away any chance of a response.

"Please," I urge, grasping for any sign that she's still connected to this world.

"Jordan... I-I killed him," she says.

I struggle to keep my professional composure while the nurse watches. "Jessica, we can work through this together," I say, forcing myself to sound hopeful.

But as I look into her anguished eyes, I know that for now, she remains tethered to this world by only the thinnest thread.

Jessica's body rocks back and forth, her eyes fixed on the past's grim shadows that dance before her eyes.

From the doorway, two other doctors arrive and observe Jessica, their concern etched on their faces as they discuss her lack of progress. They exchange theories and potential adjustments to her treatment plan, but deep down, we all know that there's no simple solution for the complex web of trauma, manipulation, and grief that has ensnared her mind.

And that's the way I want her to stay.

"Dr Scott," one doctor calls to me. "We need to discuss her medication. It's not having the desired effect."

"Understood." I steal one last glance at Jessica before stepping away from the room.

As I join the group, we delve into possibilities for alternative approaches. We argue, debate, and weigh the pros and cons of every option, minds racing with urgency. But every suggestion seems to circle back to the same haunting question: how can we break through the walls that Jessica has built round herself? Walls that I played a part in constructing.

"Maybe electroconvulsive therapy could help?" suggests one doctor, igniting another round of heated discussion. The thought of subjecting Jessica to such a procedure interests me.

For now, the flicker of life behind Jessica's eyes is the only thing that proves she remains attached to this world at all. As I grapple with the knowledge of my role in her suffering, I vow to do everything to keep her there. But the truth remains—maybe someday, the correct treatment will help bring Jessica's mind back from its devastating exile, and that is something I hope never happens.

Better she has bars around her sanity than I have bars around my freedom.

As the other doctors move to other patients, I'm left standing in the corridor outside Jessica's room, deep in thought. The wallpaper peels at the edges, and the faint scent of antiseptic hangs in the air. It's mealtime, and an orderly pushes a trolley past me, its wheels squealing like nails on a blackboard.

"Here's her dinner and medications, Dr Scott," the young man says with a sigh. His eyes betray his own weariness, a consequence of bearing witness to countless patients trapped in their own chaotic minds. "She hasn't touched anything since breakfast."

"Thank you," I reply. He hands over the tray of bland food and arranged pills.

"Maybe today will be different," he says, a hint of hopefulness in his tone as he shuffles away. But I know better.

I knock on the door before entering. "Here's your dinner, Jessica." I place the tray before her. Her gaze remains locked onto the wall, unresponsive and distant. "Jessica, eat something. They're trying everything they can to help you, but I don't think you need these yet." I slip her pills into the pocket of my trousers.

As the evening sets in, it's time to leave, and as I gather my things, the piercing sound of Jessica's screams echo down the corridor. Her frequent nightmares drag her back to the tragic accident that shattered her world, a relentless tormentor that refuses to release its grip.

I check the coast is clear before I unlock the door and step into Jessica's room, my heart heavy with the burden of my past transgressions. The dim light casts eerie shadows on her motionless form as she sits, staring at the wall. Her hair hangs limp and lifeless round her hollowed cheeks.

"Jessica," I begin, trying to break through the near-catatonic state that has consumed her. "I'm glad you're safe now. I'm going to give you a new medication. It will help keep you stable, compliant, and calm."

As I speak, memories of my role in Jordan's death slither through my mind. The hit-and-run. My actions on that fateful day. I hit Jordan, but I didn't stop because I was over the limit. I couldn't afford to jeopardise my career at the local hospital. It was me who found myself best placed to treat Jessica the day after they brought her in with shock, her vulnerability leaving her subconscious open to my manipulations and suggestions.

The Perfect Nanny

False memory can be a powerful thing I remind myself as I stare at the tortured young woman. In the hands of someone unscrupulous, it can plant experiences that never occurred, especially in those who are highly suggestible after suffering a terrible tragedy. Jessica was the perfect vulnerable patient with a history of over-compliant or highly suggestible behaviour. During our sessions, I coached Jessica to create an experience, as if in memory, that never actually happened. Putting the blame on Lucy got me off the hook. After all, who would the authorities believe? A respected psychotherapist or a child suffering from shock?

My thoughts waver, betraying the guilt that gnaws at me. "I took advantage of your vulnerable state, Jessica, and for that, I am sorry, but it was a necessity. You see, I was offered a very lucrative private partnership with several prominent psychotherapists. In fact, I was on my way back from signing the deal when I hit Jordan. I'd stopped off to celebrate and knew I was over the limit, but I had to leave the scene. Staying would have been career suicide and my name taken off the door at the exclusive Harley Street practice, where our clients are TV celebrities, pop artists, and millionaires. I couldn't and wouldn't let anything or anyone get in the way of that opportunity."

But I wonder if she's heard any of that, as she remains trapped in her agonising memories, deaf to my confession and the remorse that laces my words. As a doctor, I swore an oath to do no harm; yet here stands the evidence of my betrayal, etched onto every line of Jessica's gaunt face.

"You got away from me, and I can't have that. There's no prospect of you getting better, at least not one I can allow. There's too much of a risk that you'll discover the truth one day. So, I need you here where I can keep an eye on you. And as long as you keep taking the meds I give you, you'll be fine, and I'll keep you safe."

I step back towards the door and study her. Nothing. "I'll see you soon, Jessica."

Subscribe to my newsletter and receive your FREE ebook of *The Unwelcome Guest* that's only available to my VIP reader group:
SIGN UP HERE

CURRENT BOOK LIST

Current book list
>Hop over to my website for a current list of books: https://aaronquinnbooks.com/books/

OTHER WAYS TO STAY IN TOUCH

Other ways to stay in touch

Other ways you can connect with me:

Facebook: Aaron-Quinn Author

TikTok: Aaron Quinn Author

Email aaron@aaronquinnbooks.com with any questions, ideas or interesting story suggestions. Hey, even if you spot a typo that we've missed, then drop me a line!

ABOUT THE AUTHOR

I live in Essex in the UK and love spending time people watching and wandering the fields and forests of my county.

Before my writing career, I worked in HR within the Financial Services Sector, and then retrained as Mind Coach, before becoming a full-time author in 2015. I've always been fascinated by people, how the mind works, and the raw emotions that drive us to do the things we do.

I write dark, gripping, domestic thrillers about ordinary people in extraordinary situations. In fact, the very same people who live next door to you, or you say hi to every day. Have you ever wondered what goes on behind closed doors? Well perhaps I can enlighten you through my books.

When I'm not writing, at the gym, or playing with the 4 Yorkies in our family, you'll find me people-watching and imagining what kind of life they *really* lead.

Printed in Great Britain
by Amazon